G000048014

The light within Atlantis

By Sharon Milne Barbour

The light within Atlantis

Copyright © 2019 by Sharon Milne Barbour - Bengalrose
Healing
Published by Bengalrose Healing
Designed by Sharon Milne Barbour
Author - Sharon Milne Barbour
Book cover illustration – by CIMBart
Editors – Author and Di Reed

All rights are reserved. No part of this book may be reproduced by
any mechanical, photographic, or electrical process, or in the form of
a phonographic recording, nor may it be stored in a retrieval system,
transmitted, or otherwise be copied for public or private use - other
than for "fair use" as brief quotations embodied in articles. The
verses can be read to private or public audience. Reviews not to be
written without prior written knowledge of the publisher and author.
The intent of the author is only to offer information of a general
nature to help you on your spiritual path. In the event you use any of
the information in the book for yourself, which is your right, the
author and the publisher assumes no responsibility for your actions.

ISBN- 9781792909054

History creates legends, legends create myths and myths create a story...

The history of Atlantis has created many legends across the universe. Many beings have tried to seek the source of the Atlantean power to create their own utopias. The crusaders of the universe will be following the quest created from the myths, many failing as the true Atlantean power will for some always be just out of their reach.

The successful explorer will find the true Atlantis when they find their true self. This will be a discovery of personal magnitude and the realisation of the true Atlantean spiritual path. The seeds of Atlantis are in your earth DNA; it is in all of you, waiting to be pollinated by an unseen unconditional love energy source. When this seed is ignited, that is when you will find your true Atlantis and utopia.

This story will guide you to the Atlantean source, which will lead to an existence of wonders and miracles, but also the struggles that a utopian society can face in the reality of that time when love is lost. Please read on and remember your Atlantean seed within is ready to be triggered. It is now time for you to grow and find your utopia.

My life journal

Home planet Diacurat

Life journal section – 'The light within Atlantis'

Transmissions begin…

Life Journal – transmission 1 –
'The light within Atlantis'

Welcome to this section of my life journal 'The Light of Atlantis'. For your understanding in this translation into your language and existence frame matrix my main life journal is a mind communication transmission recording of what I choose to relay about my life. It is available for all to tap into and learn from my life journey which will help guide future generations.

Only the chosen beings selected by the Intergalactic Council can access this section of my journal on the information on Atlantis. When you connect to this journal the words of my language will be translated to all your levels of understanding, based on the dimensional existence you inhabit. Higher ascended capability beings with thought mind control will be able to download this section of my journal to their minds and technology for future knowledge purposes; for others, it is available in their printed language.

The reason I have chosen to start a separate journal section for this next phase of my life is that I just have been chosen to do something that is an amazing privilege for my planet, family and self. I want this event to stand out in my life journal, as it will go into our learning libraries and the universal knowledge pot. I know that whatever the outcome of this new adventure, it will bring great knowledge after my physical life phase has ended on my home planet.

Now I had better introduce myself, as the off-world beings reading this section of my journal will not know who I am! You are reading this part of the life journal by Touliza. My home planet is Diacurat, based in a galaxy fourth galactic quadrant in the Coma Berenices, within the prime universe of Delta. Our planet lies on one of the outer spirals with our light star. We have three moons and there are seven other planets that revolve round our light star as well, but only ours has intelligent life form. I will have great pleasure in describing my home planet through these transmissions, so please be patient with me as my story unfolds.

I have to be honest – my light day started as any other. The gentle crystal lights came on in my resting chamber and I heard my mother's voice in my head: "Touliza, it is time to rise and start your light day." My mother, Trizian, was nearly always my alarm call; I shot bolt upright when I heard her say, "And your father has been called to the highest council elders unexpectedly!"

I was now wide awake, as you did not get suddenly summoned to the council unless there was new planetary or galactic council news of great importance. My father, Holhfen, was a high-ranking member of the Diacurat Sacred Light Council. His role was one of diplomacy and facilitator to off world beings, and he also knows many languages of the Galactic planets and realms. This made him a very useful member of the Sacred Light Council and an ambassador of our planet, helping with new species contacts and their languages.

I jumped up off my resting platform and asked for the light to come in. As the window appeared I could not see the light star and lilac skies through the dome, but instead an amazing phenomenon of auras and clouds we call Zelicann. I was surprised my mother had not mentioned this, as its occurrence affects not just our planet's energies, but us as individuals. But I guess that like me she was preoccupied with why my father had been summoned for an unscheduled meeting with the Sacred Light Council.

I stood there for quite a while watching and studying Zelicann, as this was part of my field of study and interest – energies. It had arrived a bit early and it must have come in overnight; on average they happen every 100 light days or so, and usually last anything from five to ten light days. When it has dispersed, the sky returns to the familiar lilac colour, giving a clear backdrop that enables us to see our beautiful landscape, moons and light star again. The light show and swirling colours of the clouds is quite hypnotic and took my mind back to our planet's past, when my race chose to live underground when these light shows first appeared. Zelicann sends energy bursts to the surface of the planet and it is not safe to be in the storms. The positive outcomes of this phenomenon are unique plant life and minerals. It was triggered by a shift in one of our moons after an asteroid hit it. The moons affect the weather patterns on our planet, so when this one was disrupted it caused this new weather system. As well as affecting the weather pattern it also it affected the energies of the planet, plant life, creatures and the Diacuratians.

This was over a ten thousand hyons ago and as we ascended in mind and technology we built beautiful cities, half underground with large biosphere dome covers for protection. They are scattered around the planet and the domes create the biosphere of existence of balanced pure energy for us to live in. We have also received help from the other civilisations that are part of the Intergalactic Council, and they have helped us develop our technology to where we are now, aiding our development and survival. The best way for me to explain about our planet is that we live in two ecosystems, one below ground and one above, creating the best harmonious existence we can with our planet.

We do adventure to the surface of the planet to enjoy its beauty and to collect the minerals and plant life we require and to monitor the animal life. There are protected dwellings on the surface too, to use when it safe to do so on our planet's surface. We also have science stations for observation of our planet and solar system. I must not forget the star ship stations, which lie above the planet and on one of our moons, for the use of our own ships and those of visitors. Some visitors travel by star ship, while others use the light way portals, which are light and sound frequency tunnels that travel through the dimensions. They take you to your destination when you set the intent of your mind to the right frequency of the portal.

My mother was asking me to stop daydreaming and to get ready for the light day ahead, which brought me back to reality. I was visiting the science chambers today to help work on some energy projects; I knew we would be looking at the phenomenon of auras and clouds to monitor any energy changes formed since the last time they appeared, and how these could affect our ecosystems.

The reason I am so excited at the end of this light day is because when I finished my work, my mother and father were waiting for me at home. As I am usually the first to arrive home, my energy flipped thinking something was wrong. But they were all smiles and their body energies were singing out to me. They sat me down and said I had been selected for incarnation into the last phase of the Atlantis experiment. I was taken aback, my mouth dropped, and for once, my mind was silent.

Life Journal – transmission 2 –
'The light within Atlantis'

I did not get much rest last night, mainly as my news had travelled fast after my mother and father told me of my selection for the Atlantis experiment. My friends were filling my head with their excitement and questions I could not answer yet. But I managed even through my own excitement to take control of my mind and switch them off. For those of you that do not know much about us, we are telepathic and we mainly use our highly advanced minds to communicate with each other, although we also have face-to-face spoken communication. We have energy screen technology; the screens materialise in thin air as we can control the molecular structure of materials and switch on and off as needed with our thoughts. We can download images and thoughts for others to view through frequencies set for these crystal-based screens. Our minds trigger all our technologies, as we are attuned to the planet energy power source. We can also control our telepathic mind to choose whom we listen to, when and where, and it has taken hyons of discipline for our race to achieve this.

I think it will help you to understand future transmissions if I quickly explain how we make decisions on Diacurat. I mentioned the Sacred Light Council, which is one of two councils that oversee our planet; the other is the off-world Intergalactic Council. The Sacred Light Council is made up of Diacuratian ascended light masters, light priests and priestesses. They all have the power to project their minds across great distances, linking with their own kind and other species in the universe. These Diacuratians have given over their lives to this purpose to make sure we stay in the pure love energy we now inhabit, living for the one and the good of all.

They meditate every light day, focusing on the pure energy of the planet and the energy of the universe. With each generation their consciousness energy and knowledge grow, and are passed to all Diacuratians. All Diacuratians strive for this ascension; we know from other species that have achieved full ascension that they no longer need the physical body; they have ethereal multidimensional bodies with pure conscious energy. As part of the Sacred Light Council, we also welcome visitors from other planets and realms, who stay with the council and live among us for a short while, giving further teachings, guidance and support to our planet.

Our planet has qualified for this guidance as we have reached ascension level of the fifth dimension, so that some of us can detach from our physical bodies if we choose. Others are working on this ascension level and we estimate that in five more generations, all the Diacuratians will have achieved this level.

The overseers created the Intergalactic Council. They are from a divine source of pure bliss, unconditional love and light in the tenth to twelfth dimension energy realms, energy beings beyond anything you could ever imagine. They have energy form, hierarchy, and their own overseers. Compared to Diacurat, with our more limited vision and energy existence, their reality is beyond anything you will ever see here. To the lower third dimension energy planets in the universe, where this divine source has chosen to touch them with their light, they are seen as gods. If we look at our own planet's history, we find that we thought the same a long time ago. But now as we understand them more, they do not want to be worshipped, just listened to, so they can be a guiding hand for all.

The overseers created the Intergalactic Council for the purpose of bringing all ascended beings they had helped and guided together as one. The council oversees the contact of new species, guiding all species to work together in unity, and guiding those selected along the ascension path of light. Each species that is at this level of consciousness selects members of their own high council to sit on the Intergalactic Council. This council then supports the work of the overseers through the universe Delta and beyond.

As I was on my resting platform, tracing the star patterns above my head on the ceiling, I was wishing my brother Alechoian was here to be part of this family excitement. He is five hyons older than me, a handsome, bright Diacuratian with a thirst for adventure, which led him to join our light star space corps. His first ship duty was on a science ship, which was to explore the universe and carry out missions to other planets. Four hyons ago, his star ship lost contact with our planet communicators and has not been seen since. No other Intergalactic star ship has come across them either. All we know from their transmissions is that they were exploring a region of the universe called Trigidian, and a solar system that had three stars. One of the stars was unstable and nearing its end of life, so they wanted to see what information they could gather. The area around it was very unstable and the fabric of space was disrupted and creating holes. These tears in the energy can lead to other universes or dimensions and the master scientists believe that his star ship had been caught up in one of them. Although we do not feel his life force anymore, that does not mean he's dead; we hope he still exists in another place and that the crew of the star ship will one light day find its way home.

I carried on pondering my life. I was in my twenty-second hyon, a young adult now among my people; I had completed my education and was top of my class. Since birth, my destiny was to become, like my mother, a high council priestess of great standing in the Sacred Light Temple. I am ascended from a long line of light masters, and chosen children from an ascended master will be future members of the Sacred Light Council. But this does take hyons of study and dedication to achieve. In my studies I had specialised in energies of beings, planets and dimensions, taking in many species and planets including Earth's past, where the Atlantis experiments are being held. The special thing about my ability is that I can look into the past of all species. With further training, I will be able see the projected future of all species, and outcomes of their actions as my consciousness expands.

I felt that everything I had learnt so far in my life had led to this moment. I did not have to choose this assignment, as we have free will – but who in their right mind would not want to blend with a humanoid of high ascension DNA and experience this amazing time on Earth as an observer from within?

I kept my thoughts to myself as I went through this light day; I decided to take a light day for myself, as a chance to reflect. I played with my friend Dolso, a lovely, friendly animal who is very devoted to me. He's a big, clumpy, hairy thing with eyes like saucers and a smile that would light up any dull energy space. I was mesmerised by his fur, which was very black with purple and blue running through it; it swung as he moved and shimmered in the light. He is a very energetic animal, bounding around on his four legs without a care in the world, and I love his energy. He did not come from our own planet; he came from the Sirius region of the universe. When one of the

Lemurian ships came, they had younglings of Dolso species called Holpernos aboard their star ship. They are very domesticated, loving, changeling physical energy forms and they gave me one as a present when they met my father. A changeling life form can adapt to different atmospheres and sustain itself in almost any environment, so they are very useful animals for many species that travel the universe. Even as a young child, I was often included in these social meetings my father had, which included lower-level ascension beings, as my future was on the council. My father did this to ensure I grew up with respect for all species of all ascension levels and developed clarity of understanding and empathic behaviour towards them.

When my parents returned home later I told them I had accepted the assignment. They were overjoyed; I could see the pride in their eyes and their love for me. But I was not just doing this for myself; I know I will learn many wonderful things from it but it will also help many other beings, the Intergalactic Council, and all those who follow me. And as I am a scientist at heart, experiments are part of my way of learning and hard to resist!

Life Journal – transmission 3 -
'The light within Atlantis'

So the journey began, once my acceptance of the offer to be involved in the Atlantis experiment was received I was invited to the Sacred Light Council to speak with the elders and to be allocated a mission team that would work with me and over see this important mission to earth planet Gaia.

I journeyed to this meeting with my father; it was to be held in the Sacred Light Temple. We have our own flying ship, which looks like a beautiful large clear crystal ball, and allowed us to see all the beauty around us as we travelled to our destination. We were allocated a landing pad to the side of the temple; to enable us to leave our ship we would telepathically ask the crystal form to clear a space for our exit in its walls. This is achievable as we are attuned to all living things. Everything is energy and has life and intelligence; it's a case of attuning to the right frequency to ask for assistance.

We were greeted at the entrance by the Light High Lord Priest himself, Algaster, which really underlined the importance of the mission I was to undertake. We were led to a side chamber where the council was gathered, a more informal setting than I had expected. The main council chamber has twelve thrones raised up on a high platform with smaller seating areas around them, and I had expected our meeting would take place there. I soon realised they had chosen a more relaxed setting so I was not overwhelmed. I was introduced to my team members – twelve light master members of the Intergalactic Council who all had experience in the Atlantis experiment. Three of the beings that would assist: were from Pleiadian, Andromeda and Arcturian. My main point of contact was to be Telcarian, the

Pleiadian who would head up the team for my mission to Atlantis.

I discovered that Telcarian comes from the stellar system surrounding the Pleiades – seven stars existing in the fifth to ninth dimensions. His people populate three planets in the Pleiades; they can travel in light star ships and are able to switch from one dimension to another, using the light way portals to travel the universe. They are of humanoid appearance, with very pale skin and hair, through lack of pigment. They are a beautiful people and a truth race – they cannot lie, their logic and wisdom is amazing, and they see all as it should be, in the light of unconditional love. There is no negativity with these beings, a simple glance or graceful gesture can put you at ease and take away any doubts you have of what lies ahead. They are multidimensional beings, they can take on physical form when they choose to, and can teleport through the universe and materialise somewhere else with a single thought. During teleportation the cellular structure of the ethereal or physical body breaks down to an energy stream at atomic level, linking with the light way portals that allow light particle travel through space.

I was also introduced to Ioliismiem, who is also part of the mission team. He is from a fifth dimensional planet, Arcturus, in the Arcturian star system. These beings are similar to the Pleiadian and can also travel in light star ships; they can exist in the various dimensions of the universe, and are able to switch from one to another as needed when they travel the universe. Their planet is similar to the Earth planet Gaia I mentioned, and they call Arcturus the blue planet. The Arcturians are a tall race with humanoid form, over-sized joints, and an elongated skull. They dress in long robes and seem to glide rather than walk. Their smooth, blue, scaly skin shimmers as they move and are very beautiful to observe. They are a race of great wisdom and bring very logical, practical minds to the mission while maintaining their high spiritual status.

Then there was Catelifon, a female of the species from Andromeda, a planet in the Andromedan spiral – a huge galaxy, I was told, with many species of different level life forms, and the Andromedans being amongst those of the highest of intelligence. They remind me of the humanoid species, smaller and with finer features. Like the others they can exist in two forms in the third to ninth dimensions, living a mix of multidimensional and physical existence. They travel the cosmos, bringing their teachings to all of those who will listen. They are peacemakers and great mentors for the planets in the process of ascension. The Andromedans have already been part of Earth's history before the Atlantis experiments started, and continue to observe the planet. Because of their knowledge they will be a great asset to this mission.

Pleiadian, Andromeda and Arcturian are guardians of many planets at the moment, helping to protect them and ascend into the fourth and fifth dimensions of reality by helping to raise their vibration frequencies. They stand as the guardians and protectors of higher consciousness in the universe.

I think at this point I should explain about the dimension energies I have mentioned for those of you that do not yet understand them. Every frequency level of energy in the third, fourth and fifth dimensions and beyond has its own reality and celestial levels, to which your multidimensional self can adapt. As you move through the different levels, your consciousness adapts, expands and raises its frequency to that reality. This for example is what the Pleiadians, Andromedas and Arcturians have achieved, and we as a race are starting to do so as well.

A Dimension, sometimes called a Realm, is a state of consciousness and a means of organising different planes of existence according to the vibratory rate of everything that exists. Each dimension has certain sets of laws and principles that are specific to the frequency of that dimension. Dimensions are different states of being interconnected with a light grid matrix of the universe and beyond, pulsating, waving, wondrous movements of sound, colour and form. Those who resonate with a particular level of energy, which refers to their vibration and light quotient, exist in that dimension.

I am also going to add information about the dimensions for those who link into this journal and have limited understanding of them. This is key information to help you understand how the universe works, and my mission ahead.

The first dimension is the consciousness of physical prime of any physical matter. This is the dimension of, for example, minerals, and is the slowest in terms of vibratory rate. Diacurat and many other planets we know are made up of atoms, molecules and minerals. These planets are alive, radiating a frequency in this dimension. They can hold their history and knowledge that we seek, and depending on their level of consciousness, the beings that live on these planets will be able to tap into the knowledge the planet can reveal to them. All planets start at this frequency level but they can grow in energy and frequency, and ascend to fifth dimensional levels. This can take a long time to happen and usually occurs when the beings on the planet also ascend. But what is achieved can easily be reversed if the beings falter in the fifth dimensional way of being and cause harm to the planet they are part of. This can cause a shock wave to the heart of the planet's energy and frequency, triggering it to self-cleanse and purify. Higher ascended beings can connect to their planet and hear its story and wishes; these beings will work for the good of their planet and not cause it any harm.

The second dimension is simply another step that sacred consciousness takes in its rate of vibration and intent. This is the plane of plants, trees, animals and insects. One must remember that everything is alive and has an intelligence that speaks from all parts of existence. Some planets have been populated with second dimensional life from other planets, acting as the food source when populated with physical forms. In the lower energy dimension these plants and animals know their purpose – for example, to be consumed as a food source. All they ask is for thanks for their spirit, which has given this life-sustaining source, and respect for their kind and habitat. They have an intuitive sense that enables them to understand the different roles of each other and the planet they live on. This second dimension level can also ascend with a planet, alongside beings raising their frequency. Many ascended planets have beautiful, spiritual animals that are sometimes used to populate lower energy planets to help raise the energies. When an animal is of higher ascension they will no longer be a food source and will be treated as equals by the physical forms on these ascended planets; we have reached this level of ascension on Diacurat.

The third dimension is known as the physical reality of the conscious being. The third dimension is heavy, a busy, chattering, flowing dimension; beings in this dimension can hold love and kindness but also be full of fear, anger and feelings of powerlessness; many feel lost in the world they live in. They feel they want to do more for their world, but are swimming against a heavy current, living in hope the tide will change and their world will know peace. Often, these lower energy worlds know war and self-destruction, which is sad for the rest of the universe to witness.

In this dimension, the beings create their reality through their own mind restrictions – hate attracting hate, love attracting love – a circle that keeps repeating the same pattern unless they can see the light of a higher source existence. These beings only have to move their attention to other things to change their reality – which is where their mind is in that moment of their existence. In other words, beings attract more of the reality their attention is focused on, hate-to-hate, or love-to-love. These emotions also affect their physical body and its powers to self-heal, ascend, and love; these positive vibrations can move them out of the third dimension reality, while hate traps them in it.

The physical beings in a third dimension existence have certain characteristics that some of you from lower energy dimensions will recognise. They are egocentric and self-serving, and their actions are based on fear; they are judgmental and lack compassion. They are competitive, self-righteous, self-important and non-trusting. They also are materialistic, need security and are controlling. Their emotions are governed by their past experiences and a future they cannot see or control. On some of the planets that have been chosen for enlightenment, the physical beings have an ascension soul within them. They will experience love, kindness and empathy, which conflict with the heavy energy of the three dimensional existence.

If a third dimensional world is left with no spiritual awakening the beings exist in the lower heavier, darker energy of self-cycling ego; they do not survive long and can eventually self-destruct. I know questions will arise such as: "Do they have their own spirit to identify with?" Yes they do; we call it the essence of that being and on their death, their essence will merge back to their energy world, becoming one again with this existence. Remember that the overseers in dimension twelve record all energy from all realities; nothing is ever lost. When a lower energy form is connected to a higher energy as a soul within, then their lives are recorded and remembered by the ascended being that was connected to the lower energy physical form. As the physical form ascends into the higher spiritual way of understanding the fifth dimension – the beginning of the multidimensional process – then the spirit soul within is no longer needed. At this point, the Intergalactic Council takes over and guides the ascending species into further ascension stages, culminating in the full multidimensional form.

The fourth energy dimension is the astral plane; it is made up of celestial layers between the third and fifth dimensions and is what we call the middle ground, the stepping-stone to the fifth dimension. The fourth dimension is one of transition – it is smoother flowing, offering possibility, capabilities and clarity you cannot achieve in the lower dimensions. Its higher knowledge brings more hope for those still in the third dimension reality. Beings can find this astral plane in their dreams, or in the meditation state. Many high ascending beings will visit lower energy physical forms while they are asleep, using this fourth dimension conscious state to give them guidance, healing and messages. Incarnated souls also use this dimension for multidimensional travel with other incarnated souls.

This fourth dimension astral energy plane of hope leads the third dimensional beings away from the negative hate and anger energy towards the love energy, which prepares them for the unconditional love energy of the fifth dimension. To enter the fourth dimension astral plane, a lower level being needs to raise their energies and state of consciousness and vibration by working in the thoughts of peace, love and light.

When the physical being starts to ascend, they learn to control the ego excepting the transition from egoist karma fear-based reality to the love reality; to achieve this, they must have gone through spiritual awakening. Their consciousness expands, purging their minds of negative emotions and self-serving belief systems. They start to realise that their spiritual self is more than a physical body, aiding them to tap into the collective consciousness of the universe. Their species will become more telepathic and have out of body experiences connecting with the fourth and fifth dimensions. This is the start of an amazing change in themselves and their world.

The fifth dimension is a high frequency energy plane that exists in a permanent state of peace, bliss, love, kindness and joy. At this stage of ascension a physical being can choose to shed the physical body form, creating a multidimensional version of the light body's self. There are no time or space restraints, they exist in the here and now in unity, with no worries about past or future. No more negative thoughts stream into the mind of a being that has reached full fifth dimension consciousness. The conscious mind is quieter, allowing for telepathic skills and conscious growth; existence will be without the constant chatter that flows into the third dimension mind. While in this wonderful fifth dimension, you can also connect to the universe knowledge library and achieve so much more.

The physical forms that ascend into the fifth dimension energy are without ego and live for service to others. All their actions are based on love and their hearts and minds know only unconditional love. They recognise themselves as the whole and with this understanding, duality and linear time dissolve. There is no longer a need for possession or status. You can still be in physical form in this dimension, and if you wish, choose to let go the physical body as you ascend to the higher levels of the fifth dimension, and into sixth and seventh.

The sixth to twelfth dimensions open up to vast consciousness that increases on each level. As you enter the higher dimensions you lose shape and form. This is like an abstract painting – it can be hard to describe in a lower energy language.

The sixth dimension is where conscious ideas can begin in the language of life and light in the morphogenetic fields. These are patterns of energy that hold your template, recording the geometry of not only of your physical and ethereal bodies, but also the collective information of your species. A species' morphic field is much like a monad connecting us all genetically, culturally, and spiritually. We know that once the critical mass of that species reaches a specific high level of ascension, the rest of the species can automatically ascend in what is called a global ascension, connecting with the six dimensions. Beings that live in these dimensions are able to transform in both these dimensions and the lower energy dimensions. They can adjust to a physical state as well as living a highly ascended way of being. They can travel through dimensions and alternate realities without being seen by the lower, heavier worlds of, say, the third dimension realities. A being's mission in this dimension is to teach others about the conscious light and how to grow in each dimension so you can ascend to the next, and understand the ascension journey ahead of them.

The seventh dimension is the realm of cosmic sound, which is the harmonics of creation. The sound of creation weaves together the structure of the universe and all we know in a geometric matrix. The best way for me to explain this is if you imagine fine threads interweaving through the universe connected to everything, all creation held together by a divine vibration of harmonic sounds. Beings in the lower level dimensions cannot hear this – it is audible only when you ascend to this higher level of conscious being with no form or shape, as you grow in understanding of your worlds.

All beings have a unique signature frequency note that radiates out and links with this dimension. Highly ascended non-physical light beings work along a vibration of light and sound as their form moves in the dimensional layers of the universe. Beings in third to fifth dimensional consciousness can interpret these beings as tall light beacons or light orbs. Beings in the sixth dimension and beyond see high-ascended beings in their true light form. The seventh dimension being can also choose to appear as a physical being in their communication with lower energy civilisations, to aid their understanding of them.

The eighth dimension is the realm of conscious pure light mind energy of creation. Beings that can reach this dimension can join together, as individual cells come together to form a single body, and work together to create new wonders. This joining of the few to become one is the beginning of all possibilities; what is manifested appears in different ways, depending on your level of ascension in the universe. These beings can manifest creation for the multidimensional, non-physical reality and the solid physical planes in the first to third dimensions. If a physical being is connected to the eighth dimension, they can manifest all they need with a single thought – for example dwellings, food and clothes. A physical being in the third dimension who has not ascended beyond this point cannot manifest what they need in this way, but they can create, say, a building through physical materials by using their physical strength and intelligence. In the lower dimensions, your choices govern how this manifests in your reality.

Many species that understand the sound harmonics and pure light energy of the seventh and eighth dimensions have used this power source for light port way travel and star ships.

The ninth dimension hosts beings that exist in the multidimensional energy form. They can create star travel throughout the dimensions and can also choose to take on a physical form on a planet – or even *be* a planet! This is where the hierarchy of all form in the universe is established. For example, planets and physical beings need their light star energy source to survive, but the light star can survive without the planet and beings. From the light star to the small speck of mineral dust, all have purpose and hierarchy, once this chain of events is started, each will depend on the other for survival and all will depend on the light star.

The tenth dimension holds the living truth of all that was and will be, and is the pure light from unconditional love that is within everything. It is the backbone that runs through all dimensions, holding them together and projecting consciousness into any form in the universe with the energy of *'Intention'*. Remember that the intent behind any thought and action ripples through all the dimensions. Pure intent is a very powerful energy and it is the thoughts of a pure mind and heart that creates it. This dimension is also a gateway into other universes beyond the tenth, eleventh and twelfth dimensions. The gateway is monitored, and travel to these other universes is restricted with the understanding that all travelers must cause minimal disruption, to maintain the balance of all. The other universes also have gateways with the same understanding, which the overseers have assured across many, many existences.

The eleventh dimension is the realm of the universe's living consciousness. Here, a universe can be created, or destroyed by calling all living energy forms home to this realm. The overseers are part of this universe consciousness, bringing unconditional love pure light energy to all they choose to enlighten. They are linked closely to the tenth and twelfth dimensions as these three hold all of creation in place.

The twelfth dimension holds the nucleus of all, sitting in an energy womb that resonates out infinitely. It expands to embrace all the dimensions and galactic existence with a cosmic matrix running through all the dimensions. The number twelve is part of form through the universes – for example, some highly ascended physical beings have twelve strands of DNA. This is the pure conscious centre of all, where the overseers reside and have gateways to all existence. The beings from this dimension are extraordinary cosmic beings of

29

the purest light; only they know this bliss and pure love consciousness energy.

I hope this information has helped you. I am to go back tomorrow to the temple to sit down with my mission team, to discuss the lead up to my linking with the human form on Atlantis. I am also to be part of the decision-making process, so I understand my journey to the planet Earth and the consequences of the decisions made leading up to it.

I have spent the rest of the day with my head in a telepathic spin, a joke of course, but my energy was buzzing, so I took a walk in our beautiful outside recreational space, near my home. There I met up with some of my friends and we sang and played music and relaxed, enjoying the beautiful energy this gave us. This will help me sleep tonight to rest my busy mind for the light days ahead.

Life Journal – transmission 4 -
'The light within Atlantis'

I rose early this light day to make sure I was prepared for my meeting with my mission team members. Everything else in my life was now on hold, but I felt it was perfect timing. I had just finished my main education and had started working with the master scientists at the science chambers and looking at developing my role, which would eventually lead to being a Sacred Light Council member. This new opportunity would advance this for me and jump-start my life as part of the sacred light temple community.

I decided to sit in the home mediation chamber to clear my mind; this always helps me focus on the day a head. The meditation chamber is a beautiful crystal healing space of wonderful calming energy. Whenever I am in here, Dolso is always outside with his nose pressed against the door waiting for me to finish. He is drawn to this space during the day, and I have often found him resting in the chamber. Unfortunately, I could not risk being suddenly taken out of my deep meditation by a big wet lick and Dolso drooling all over me, so he has to stay outside.

When I had finished meditating, I cleansed my body in the light chamber and moisturised my skin, and sat in the light energy crystal lamp rays to absorb some high energy, as our light star was blocked from view with the aura cloud storm. I then took time to dress and wore my new robes; I felt it was important to create a confident presence. My long, silver-white hair was tied up in a tight plait, and I wore some simple crystal jewellery. My race is a tall one; I guess translating to your earth language measurements, in adulthood we are somewhere between seven and eight feet in height. We have pale, lilac-blue skin that varies in shade amongst our species. Over the hyons, our skin has become translucent and to most lower energy species you would see us as solid form, but see our veins pulsing. How we are seen varies on the dimensional existence of the energy being. Basically, the species' lower energy fields dictate how they perceive highly ascended beings that exist in the high frequency energies.

I am looking forward to interacting and conferring with high-ascended masters of our race and other species. I know language is no barrier as we have voice translators that our minds can tap into as needed. I am excited for the next stage of my journey and what lies ahead for my people and me.

As I reached the sacred light temple, Telcarian met me and led me to a study chamber, similar to the type of room I would use in the knowledge library where I sometimes studied. I discovered this was of a higher ascension access and from it, I could access the universal knowledge library, and could gain information and life lessons in physical bodies from across many species. I tell you I was in awe – and in my element, as I love learning. Any nerves I had turned to pure excitement as I sat back and listened to these wonderful new friends in front of me.

We all sat in a circle for easy conversation. Firstly, Telcarian explained, with others adding their knowledge, how they would achieve my connection with the physical body that will be selected for my life on Earth in Atlantis.

He explained that a lot of highly ascended species living in the fifth dimensions and higher levels were what we would recognise as ethereal bodies of form and energy. They achieved soul to body connection by separating a section of their consciousness of multidimensional self and this was used for incarnating into the human physical form. The human physical form being exists in a lower plane of the Earth's energy. The incarnated being's higher self-energy stays in their home source existence, where they are always connected and observed.

He pointed out that Diacuratians had reached the fifth dimensional level of unconditional love and now understood that the self worked for the whole. With each new generation we were accelerating this energy field and ascending the fifth dimension levels as our conscious capabilities grew. This is why we were now part of the Intergalactic Council and as a planet, were gaining our standing in the universe. Some Diacuratians have achieved existence out of the physical body in multidimensional form, returning to the physical body when needed. Now we had started this ascension process, the rest of the planet would follow over the next few generations.

As I was to be the first Diacuratian to incarnate in another species' physical form, they were going to be cautious. He explained he had already overseen a lot of species that were doing this for the first time, which was why he was here to head up my team. He will be with us until the end of my life mission on Earth. He also explained the time on Earth was different to ours – what we call a light day, which is when our light star sets and rises, is a lot longer than a light day on Earth. With one of our days equalling five Earth days, my life span on Earth would seem different. As a species, we have moved away from measuring what we do in time, living more in the now; things happen when they happen, as they should.

One of the high priests, Ulsm, explained I would stay

protected in the Sacred Light Temple during my time in multidimensional separation, enabling close family connected to the Sacred Light Temple to visit me. Once the separation is done, I will be able to move around the temple and observe my reflection of self in my incarnated Earth body, connecting as needed to my team all around me, guiding that life and my purpose there.

They explained that with the power of my mind, I will be able to connect to my reflection of self-energy in the Earth humanoid being. I noted some called this the spirit within, while on Earth it is named soul. My mind would link to the energy frequency of the Earth being and it would be as if I was observing a connection in another time and place, watching it play out. I understood what they meant because as part of my studies, I often viewed transmission journals of other past Diacuratian lives to gain knowledge, and this would be a similar experience. I have not yet had access to the universal knowledge library, but knew on my path of ascension here on Diacurat it would have just been a matter of time before it was granted. This mission had brought that opportunity to me faster.

The conclusion of the meeting was that I was to spend a few days studying knowledge of the Atlantis experiments before we reconvened.

When I got home I was literally floating around the room! I had released my multidimensional self from my physical self, with Dolos leaping around below me. This always confused him a bit and he would get over-excited. My energy was so high, but I knew I had to control myself; from now on, I need to focus and take life a little bit more seriously.

Life Journal – transmission 5 –
'The light within Atlantis'

I do believe I faced reality today. For the first time in a long time I connected with a lower energy called self-doubt. I was feeling uncertainty, as my time of separation would take me away from my friends and the physical connection of the lives I have with them. I would be able to see my parents, as they are highly ascended and part of the Light Council, and their energy is acceptable around me as I go through this experience of separation. As I sat there stroking Dolos I was concerned about being parted from him. I knew the separation was just a fraction of my life span and I would be connecting to my world and getting regular updates, but it was still food for thought. I had accepted the mission and deep inside I knew it was for the benefit of all, but the lower energy still within me had placed a seed of doubt which worried me. I was not used to feeling like this, as I usually live my life in a positive vein of thought.

I sought out my mother and told her how I felt and she, of course, fully understood my dilemma. She took me back to a time when she entered the Sacred Light Temple for ten hyons, to train in healing and meditation to expand her conscious mind, and she felt the same. She explained that doubt is one of the few heavier energies that still sits within us. She said our lesson is to rise above this negative energy, because this is how we will all ascend. She told me to go to the mediation chamber and draw on my highest and best energies, and to release all this lower non-serving energy to the universe. She also told me that animals reside in the Sacred Light Temple and they might let Dolos be there with me, especially as we had such a high-energy bond that would benefit me.

I wish you could see the Sacred Light Temple. It is a layered pyramid structure built from mineral stone and crystal. There are chambers within its walls where the Light Council meets, as well as areas for science and study. There are living resting chambers and outside garden spaces to enjoy. This temple is cocooned in a high energy that was created by the light crystal found on Diacurat. The crystal is thousands of hyons old and has pure unconditional love energy and hyons of history, wisdom and philosophy stored within it. The Diacuratians chosen to be the ascended masters among us connect to this life source and bring this knowledge to our people.

The teachings of ascended masters are about living in the now, shedding past and future worries, and bringing love and kindness to all while working together for the whole of Diacurat. This crystal is the most powerful source our planet has. We know it was given to our planet by high-ascended beings travelling the universe and dimensions in the hope of bringing change to all they meet. Their mission is to bring lower energy worlds, realms and dimensions into the higher energy of unconditional love and enlightenment. These beings are known as overseers, and some lower energy civilisations see them as gods. They are in the high-ranking spectrum in the tenth to twelfth dimension in the universe, with influence over the Intergalactic Council they created. The heads of the Council confers with the overseers for advice and confirmation they are happy with decisions made for the good of the whole.

We ourselves no longer have belief systems that worship gods, but have learnt to respect all life and take responsibility for our actions of the one, so we help all on our planet. This we have learnt from the overseers that left us many hyons ago. On Diacurat, we are a civilisation that is ascending at different stages. I am privileged amongst my people, and more highly ascended than others are, but this does not make me better than anyone else. We have an understanding that all Diacuratians have a purpose and great respect for each person and their life role, and trust the ascended masters. There are no egos on Diacurat, and the only thing I feel holding us back is that little bit of lower doubt energy that occasionally pops up – the feeling I am experiencing this light day.

After meditating in the chamber I dressed and headed off to the temple, where I asked to meet with Telcarian before I started my studies. I chose not to mention my earlier feelings of doubt, and decided to just ask about Dolso. Telcarian was very understanding and gave his permission for Dolso to reside in the temple, in my resting chambers and garden grounds, but not when I was in the working chambers of knowledge and ascension, where he would distract us.

I was shown to my study chamber and made familiar with the crystal technology that I could use to connect to the universal knowledge library, where I would be restricted to the subject areas that would help me on this mission. I understood this as a wise move, as I did not want to be distracted from the task ahead. I had a naturally curious mind, but enough restraint to know the light day would come when I could access further knowledge of great wisdom.

I accessed the information about the Atlantis experiment on Earth. There was so much to absorb that I knew it would take me a few light days. For the purpose of my journal I will add notes on each stage in my transmissions, to help you understand what has led to the fifth Atlantis experiment.

I am about to join my parents for the evening, an important time for us to catch up and see how our light days have been, and what we have learnt. Even though we are telepathic, we stay out of each other's minds unless invited. I have three-way mind chats sometimes with them, which are very interesting, knowing when the next will have thoughts to transmit. But as a race we still love the physical bonding energy of being in the same space and seeing our physical bodies' reactions to what we have to say. I've discovered that you can learn a lot from the body language of a species alone.

Life Journal – transmission 6 –
'The light within Atlantis'

I have been so busy studying, I have not had a moment to log into my journal for a few light days. But I have a lot to tell you that will help you understand the reasons behind Atlantis and the several experiment attempts that have been created.

I record my life journal by mind link to my crystal source. Diacuratians can record all our knowledge on these pure energy crystals, by setting our minds at the right frequency. Whoever in the future wishes to access my life journal simply tunes into the frequency to gain the knowledge. The same process is applied for any learning I do at the temple or knowledge library.

I have created an Earth time line for myself to help me visually see the events of Atlantis. This is based on Earth's third dimensional time frame and what they call years.

Atlantis experiments time line

250,000 BC to 52,000 BC: three experiments of Atlantis were held on Earth in this time frame.

52,000 BC: there was an extinction event on Earth, which triggered the planet to shift her axis. After this, Earth was left to settle and reacclimatise.

28,000 BC to 18,000 BC: this was the time period of the fourth Atlantis experiment.

18,000 BC: Earth has another axis shift again and a mini ice age starts.

11,500 BC: Areas of Earth were recovered enough for the fifth Atlantis experiment. The experiment has been going for 1550 Earth years at this stage of recording my life journal.

When I study any subject I always like to question what I discover, because I want to understand why the decisions were made that affected so many for so long.

So my first question was: Where did this experiment idea start?

The divine creators, the overseers, and the Intergalactic Council, with its mission to bring unconditional love and kindness to all in the universe, triggered this experiment idea. They travelled across universe Delta, to look at all lower energy realms, planets and the multi dimensions that sit within this energy level of the universe. They wanted a centre point for the experiment, which would be an exchange centre for information, a light centre of this living cosmic library of knowledge. I use the word cosmic as beings from far and wide were at intervals invited to view these experiments and gather their own observations to learn from. They would bring their knowledge back to the Intergalactic Council, the overseers, and their own civilisations.

When they found a planet that was deemed suitable – Earth – it was used to see if various high-ascended energy beings could incarnate within the physical humanoid body and maintain the high source link of the divine creative energy. The core of this was to see how information could be stored through frequencies and the genetic process. If successful, the experiment would pave the way to helping other lower energy planets and civilisations survive and thrive. They could incarnate into these beings, bringing the unconditional love energy, and wait for the spark of the pure love to be recognised, which would lead to starting the ascension process. So as you can see, there was a lot riding on the success of these Atlantis experiments.

There was great debate of how to go about this experiment. Some members of the Intergalactic Council are master geneticists; they redesigned a species called humanoids by combining DNA from different star beings and with the old humans left on Earth from previous off-world visits. They designed these adult humanoid beings as living vessels for the light high-energy of those chosen to incarnate into them. The beings that chose to incarnate would learn about how to live in a physical body and maintain a high-energy existence while doing so. If successful, this experiment would pave the way for helping the ascension of future third dimensional planets and civilisations, by enabling third dimensional bodies to adapt to a higher frequency existence and gain greater understanding of their role in the universe.

After a long time of observation, they decided to focus on one planet, Gaia, which was commonly known as Earth. This was over 250,000 Earth years ago.

The first three Atlantis experiments were between the Earth's dates 250,000 BC to 52,000 BC.

Earth was selected as it was a high-energy, beautiful planet due to its location on the fringes of its galaxy, with a stable solar system. It was close to many light way portals, which are highways for some energy forms to travel through the universe. Its position had a central energy source that radiated out, and was a good observation point for all species involved. At this time, Earth had an animal population of its own and lower level, primitive humanoid life forms sporadically placed around the planet.

The history of Earth showed previous visits by alien humanoid forms – the life we encountered on the 250,000 BC time line was the result of those left behind. They had regressed to a primitive existence, as they had had no connection to the higher source energy for a long time. Evolution was slow for this Earth population because they had only to concentrate on daily survival. Although the physical form can survive without the pure incarnated soul, its energies stay locked in the lower energy grid. Unless there is that internal spark of light leading them out of the heavier energies, the physical form cannot evolve spiritually, unless the overseers leave teachings in crystal form as they did for us. They can, however, evolve with technology and materialistic greed; through observation of these civilisations, unfortunately many on this path eventually self-destruct.

The master scientists of the Intergalactic Council created a new, highly intelligent physical humanoid species that could survive in the lower energy for the higher ascended spirit energy to incarnate into. They were similar to the humanoid primitive forms, with head, arms, legs and internal body makeup, but had star DNA, creating a physical being that could survive and sustain a host while staying connected to the highest divine source surviving in a lower energy field of a planet's second and third dimensions.

The new humanoids were tall with very pale blue grey skin, high foreheads, blue eyes and blond hair. The new DNA came from four high-ascended species in the universe compatible with the Earth humanoid DNA. It had to be from species that still took physical form, so the Lemarutarian, Pleiadian,

Arcturian and Andromedan were chosen. The DNA was already charged with high consciousness, as the aim of the experiment was to create a physical form suitable for incarnation by a highly ascended ethereal form. The chosen ones to incarnate were aware while in their physical form of their mission on Earth, to create and sustain a highly ascended utopia culture, which other ethereal beings could incarnate into. These physical human beings could live for around 150 or more Earth years and radiated out their pure energy. This was because of the healing light energy that sustains the incarnated being (known as soul or inner spirit).

When the physical life wore out or the inner spirit chose to terminate their link with the physical form, the incarnated inner spirit returned to their source home. There, they would evaluate their learning and often return, to improve on their previous life experience and lessons. It was also felt that guardians should be appointed from the various species involved, one for each human. The guardians acted as guidance messengers between the incarnated souls home world, to the Intergalactic Council and overseers.

In the first Atlantis experiment, there was no sex gender in the new Earth species; they reproduced by the conscious mind. To keep the populations going, the Intergalactic Council provided humans on Earth when required. The council wanted to keep it simple at the start, monitoring the physical body reaction to an incarnated soul. So these human beings did not know physical love as those in future experiments did. The council also chose to create the cities and living areas on a warm southern landmass. There was a well-balanced ecosystem for survival among the Earth species at the time. The Council also introduced animals from some of the incarnated home worlds

– such as winged horses and exotic flying creatures, which, as spiritual beings in their own right, were treated as equals. The Council was very keen to create a spiritual environment on Earth where there would not be much outside influence. They created a life of utopia with no materialistic values, and all actions taken were for the whole.

This new Earth human species for the first Atlantis experiment was called Lemurians, after the Lemutarians who incarnated into the new Earth beings. They were selected for this first experiment due to their study involvement on this subject. As time progressed and the first experiment proved to be a success, they also eventually selected other ethereal beings to join them, contributing to this new utopia.

From what I have absorbed from the knowledge files, it was made easy for them as they could call upon the Intergalactic Council for help at any time. They also had the individual power to manifest anything they desired – buildings, recreational areas, clothes and food. They had the ability because they were linked to the eight dimensions and called upon this high source energy to manifest; the support for building their cities and technology helped them to bond as one. All their needs were met and as far as I can see there were no challenges set, so they had no way to stretch and grow. They were telepathic and psychic and stayed for a long time connected to the divine source, living wonderful lives with a lot of help and support. Other highly evolved beings connected with the Intergalactic Council came to visit the Earth beings. Word soon got out into the universe of these experiments and caused a lot of interest, which led to curious spectators, some arriving in star ships, others by teleportation through the dimensions light way portals. The experiment was a huge success, but these new visitors influenced them over time as their thoughts and behaviour brought a different way of thinking, leaving their mark on the Atlantean society.

The Lemurian humanoids were so highly ascended it was as if even in a physical form, they were ethereal and unaware of the world around them. I feel from what I have linked to they did not even really admire the Earth they were living on – they were kind and only took what was needed to survive, but they did not connect to her as I feel they should have done. Because Earth is a living entity in her own right and should have been part of their decision-making process every day. This is because the two dimensional planet with the three dimensional Earth humans had to then adapt to the new ascended human beings energies. A planet also changes its energies and can ascend. But the Lemurians did not have this consideration as far as I can see. I think they were so caught up in the success energy of the new utopia they had created, that the true connection and meaning of the divine and their purpose started to waver and eventually lost.

I was surprised how naive these first experiments were all those years ago. As a scientist, I felt they should have been challenged more. If everything is done for you and your world is cocooned to maintain an ascended way of being, then it will be success. If you introduce challenges like creating your own homes from planet resources and physical mating, followed by caring for your young, this sets goals. Then the challenge is to carry out all these tasks while still working together as one for the whole, and maintaining the high source energy. I feel this approach would make a much better experiment and learning curve for all involved.

While the first two experiments were similar, the second phase experiment introduced mixed gender. This meant that the humanoid DNA gradually altered over time with each new generation. They were still a beautiful race of beings, living in beautiful cities within a utopia lifestyle. Earth did not pose many threats, as they fortified their boundaries to keep the outside world at bay. They had flying machines and sea boats to explore the world, not really showing any thought of how they might affect the lower energy populations if they were seen. On the plus side, the incarnated beings would be enjoying the experience of participating in these experiments and each would learn from them. As far as I can see from the knowledge preserved, change came when they allowed visits to Atlantis by other off-world beings. This brought new influences to the physical beings and changed their outlook on life. Over thousands of years the humans developed their own self-essence, developing ego and self-preservation, which led to a breakdown in this utopian society.

I also question whether the first new one gender humanoid species were created with free will, and how the incarnated being influenced their existence and decision-making. I feel that over time in the second experiment phase, the physical beings evolved to develop a strong free will, and this is what triggered them to rebel against the light source and sink into the lower energies that destroyed them.

From these first two experiments lessons were learned, and the overseers and Intergalactic Council evaluated the results to make their future decisions for a third experiment. They upped the challenge from day one and decided to again bring in new humanoids of male and female gender, to see if this helped the bonding of the human forms on a different level. These new human beings would have free will alongside the new star DNA running through their physical makeup. This time they were charged with twelve energy light points aligned above, through and below the body, which they called chakras.

I don't want to overload you with information, but I need to explain the twelve chakras to you to help you understand the human form, and the thinking behind the master scientists' decision to add these to their third experiment. The master scientists felt the male and female humanoids needed an energy centre to link the feminine and masculine energy to the higher pure light source and the pure energy of Earth.

With the new human beings of separate gender, the chakra system would help keep them focused on the higher source and be a source of healing. The earth star chakra kept them grounded in the two and three dimensional matrix, with the body chakras balancing health and mind. The higher, out-of-physical-body chakras are for the connection to the divine source, with light beings guiding them.

Chakra one – this is the *earth star chakra*, which sits below the human form. The new physical beings on Earth would have a unique connection with the Earth life force and to the crystalline matrix grid, which holds the divine light contained within the Earth.

Chakra two – they called this the *root chakra* and it is located at the base of the humanoid spine in the centre of the physical body. The root chakra is a grounding chakra, which helps individuals stay centered, secure, active, energised, and present in the moment. It also allows healing energy to flow up from the Earth and into the rest of the chakras. It is an important foundation for the seven chakras that are contained within the physical human body. The root chakra also allows the human form to experience safety and security in their life whenever there is spiritual balance.

Chakra three – this is the *sacral chakra* and is based in the human form above the root chakra at the centre of creativity and sexuality. Its function is to deal with issues of relationships and social interaction; this centre is also the dwelling place of the human's true self. The sacral chakra rules abundance, creativity, wellness and joy, and also controls passions, sex and pleasure, and brings the lesson of learning to let go.

Chakra four – this is the *solar plexus chakra*; it sits above the sacral chakra and is the power centre which stores energy – a key chakra for all the chakras to function correctly. The solar plexus is the centre of will, and it controls issues from the past as well as ambitions and goals for success in the future. This is the centre of an individual's personality, and its state of balance is directly correlated to their sense of willpower, self-acceptance, and their ambition to succeed.

Chakra five – this is the *heart chakra*, located in the centre of the human over the beating heart, and is where the emotional inner being and the physical and spiritual meet. The heart controls relationships, and when the chakra is open, it allows the love energy to flow through the human being able to relate to others with love and compassion. The heart chakra also allows individuals to be empathetic to the feelings and emotions of others, while remaining true and in tune with their own energy and self. The human heart spiritual base is designed for the heart to help with emotional healing, with love for self and others, as well as overseeing self-appreciation of beauty, and willingness for compassion. The heart chakra is a sacred portal, which gives access to the gifts of your higher energetic centres, and is the doorway to the realms to source and divine love.

Chakra six – this is the *throat chakra* and is the human being's communication centre. It is the centre of truth, personal expression, listening, responsibility, faith and creativity. The way the voice is used is overseen by the throat chakra, through singing, communicating, talking and listening. When opened and balanced, the throat chakra allows humans to speak their truth of their divine love purpose.

Chakra seven – this is the *third eye chakra* and is located in the centre of the human forehead. It is the centre of psychic ability and also plays a role in feeling, sensing, and hearing connection to all in the universe. This chakra also connects human energies to beyond the physical form, linking individuals with the subconscious mind and the higher realms of high ascension energy. The third eye chakra oversees learning, memory, telepathy, clairvoyance, mediumship and aura sensing.

Chakra eight – this is the *crown chakra* and is on the crown of the head, connecting the human being to the higher spiritual realms through the higher chakras. When it is awakened it connects to the mind's dreams, visions, hopes, spiritual downloads, and alignment with their higher self-purpose. When the crown chakra is open, humans are linked to the unconditional love of the divine source, which then opens up all possibilities in their lifetime.

Chakra nine – is the *soul star chakra*. Chakras nine to twelve sit in line with the other chakras above the human form. When these are activated, it allows the divine light to flow through this energetic centre to access higher consciousness. It flows up to the divine source and then back down to the chakras and physical body to replenish, empowering and enlightening. It gives access to unconditional love which can be truly felt and experienced, bringing awareness of the power of the soul within the physical form, enabling spiritual being to be recognised. The soul star chakra acts as a flowing river of soul energy and contains the accumulated soul experiences that can be accessed for divine purpose.

Chakra ten – is the *spirit chakra* and when opened, will allow the human being to link to the expansive realms of highly ascended beings. It guides them to remember their direct connection with the divine source, and their ability to communicate with light beings, such as angels, guides, and star beings from around the universe. When this chakra is activated, the human willingly surrenders to the flow of spirit, allowing the divine source to flow into the human experience of existence and connect with the incarnated spirit within. This enables the full extent of the incarnated soul's abilities to be accessed, along with the realisation of their expansive ability to create, which is empowered through the direct connection to divine source.

Chakra eleven – This is the *universal chakra* and represents all that is in the universal energy flow. This chakra is also the access point to the doorway that opens the infinite flow of creation. When this chakra is activated the human feels in close alignment to the universe and all that is. It also allows for their divine light body to be fully constructed, the multidimensional being which then allows unlimited access to travel within the higher realms of spirit through light way portals.

Chakra 12 – is the *galactic chakra* and is the frequency to the light portals that travel beyond the limits of light harmonic sound and space, teleportation, instant manifestation and bi-location – the ability to be in more than two places at a time. When connected, the activated human can reach anywhere in the realms of creation, communicate with the highest vibration light beings and ascended masters, including the womb of creation. This also activates healing, insight and growth from the highest light realms into their existence.

If you take the time, you can see the link between the twelve chakras and the twelve dimensions explained earlier. Everything is connected, and the chakras were designed to link with these higher energy sources when activated. For the human being to be in a high state of frequency and stay connected to the unconditional love divine light source, all twelve chakras must be activated. If their energy drops the chakras will start to waver, but healing can regenerate them. If the human form drops into a lower energy, the chakras nine to twelve will shut down, breaking the source link. The crown chakra and third eye chakra will also shut, leaving the other chakras to function in the physical body form alone. The rest of the open chakras will then become under energised and the human body will then experience disease and pain.

With the mixed genders, the master scientists chose to guide the third experiment humans, connecting the volunteer souls so they found their soul mate. They decided some should stay single for the roles of priest and priestess in the light temples, and that these humans would be more highly evolved with greater consciousness. The physical bonding love was seen as an act of pure connection, with the result of new life to be highly valued. Again, this was all overseen by the Intergalactic Council, which influenced the DNA of these people born to Earth. The humans this time round were also highly intelligent, but the DNA was diversified to produce individual beings as opposed to the identical beings of the first experiment. The plan was that human appearance would become more varied than the second experiment through the new generations.

In each of the three experiments, some of the human forms developed strong egos, and this energy affected the incarnated souls as time passed. The soul was still connected to the divine source, but the human ego lost sight of the mission, and their energies became heavier. Over time, humans realised their own powers could influence others of their race, and an avaricious way of being came about, resulting in a materialistic, greedy reality. With each new generation, the humans distanced themselves from the high-energy pure unconditional love source and their powers weakened. Some of the humans developed ego and self-survival, seeing others as threats.

In the third experiment the higher chakras I mentioned earlier started to shut down. Eventually, the Atlantean culture split into two halves, one half descending into lower energies. This led to more division among the lower energies forms, which led to self-destruction through war in the three experiments. The Intergalactic Council then cleared the Earth of this self-destruction and let it settle, before another experiment attempt.

It came to the point where many of the incarnated beings in

humans, who were still in the high energy, did not wish to stay on Earth, because they knew it would end in destruction. So they were given the choice to finish their experience in the human form on Earth, or vacate the physical body and return to their home existence. Many did choose to leave the experiment. This, combined with the breakdown of the rest of the Atlantean society, contributed to the failure of the first three Atlantis experiments, with all ending in similar fates.

In the latter stages of these experiments, the ethereal beings who left the physical bodies when they were dying, had to heal and evaluate what went wrong when they got back home. They were also chosen to reincarnate for the fourth experiment, in the hope that the lessons were learnt and mistakes would not be repeated. Some lower energy Atlantean humans survived the wars and carried on living on Earth, connecting with the other lower energy human beings developing on the planet. As a side experiment, they were allowed to live out their lives in these small pockets of civilisation. Their DNA mixing with the Earth humanoid forms made them more intelligent and advanced in their thinking, and the more primitive humans saw these new beings as gods. This was because even though they had declined into the lower energies, they were of different appearance and intelligence. We observed that humans in the lower energy saw anything they did not understand as something to worship, through fear of the unknown.

Each time an experiment self-destructed, the Council left a time period of settlement before trying again. Two failed attempts followed by a third caused the overseers to put a stop to these experiments for a while, and ask the Intergalactic Council to revaluate what it was trying to achieve. After the destruction of the cities the third experiment ended with allowing an asteroid to hit the Earth, triggering an extinction event; they felt it was time to re-cleanse the planet and let her be for a few thousand years to find her pure frequency again.

I have to admit I was struggling to understand why. But who am I to question these highly ascended beings? On the other hand, I have free will, and expressing my thoughts is natural to my scientific mind. I felt it was playing with lives; the human forms eventually had their own essence, which eventually broke down into an egotistic form, creating the karma energy, pain, hate and anger which led to self-destruction – a primitive way of being we still see on under-developed worlds in the lower energies. I guess it was fascinating for the pure energy ethereal beings to experience and learn from, but I feel it took too long to stop and I was surprised that the Intergalactic Council was knowingly harming a beautiful planet. These are questions to ask when I have learned more on the subject. This might sound quite a statement to make as I have already agreed to part take in the experiment, but my mind likes to evaluate and question as I progress on the learning journey ahead.

Life Journal – transmission 7 –
'The light within Atlantis'

Still my studies continue! As you can imagine, I am very distracted with all this new knowledge at the moment. When I have finished this study period I will have a couple of light days to digest it all and reflect. I am missing Dolso and my friends, but I will have to get used to the latter for now and my foreseeable future.

I don't actually move into the temple until the mission training starts. So at the moment I am away from my home and Dolso in the light day periods. I would love to have him with me as I study but as Telcarian said, he would be a distraction. He seems to be coping, as my very good friend Zogica is visiting him to play when he can. I have known Zogica a long time; he is the same age as me but such a different character. He is very creative in his thinking and is a designer of our homes and future architecture. He works with his father in creating their own architectural ideas, or developing chamber structure designs from their own and clients' thoughts.

Before I get distracted again, here is some further knowledge from my studies on Atlantis for you to help you understand my mission.

The fourth Atlantis experiment – 28,000 BC to 18,000 BC

The Intergalactic Council decided again that the physical human would be created in male and female form, reproducing through physical contact. They also decided that life would not be as comfortable as in previous experiments, which made the fourth Atlantis experiment more of a challenge. The humans were downloaded with the practical skills of survival, but also with the psychic energy needed that would give them a chance to achieve oneness with each other and the Earth. Their DNA was similar to that of the third experiment, but this time they added some new strands from the light beings of Salcariton. The DNA can alter in regenerations of the physical forms to higher or lower frequencies, depending on the species' development. The ascended masters could switch off the frequencies if they wanted a lower energy being, and turn them up if they required a being with higher energy frequency. So they conducted trials to try and find a suitable balance in each experiment. They hoped they had it right this time. The new Earth humanoid also had the 12 chakras to help maintain the physical and mind connection to the divine source and the planet.

The Salcaritons were from the ninth dimension, raised above the Sirius region of the universe – another high-ascended ethereal race that the overseers invited to the fourth experiment. When not in physical form, their DNA is what we call star DNA, an injection of their ethereal energy. These spiritual beings existed in a blissful heavenly utopia plane of oneness in unconditional love. Their reality is on 64 levels, with ascension levels sitting within these. They have high-ascended masters, pure angelic energy beings and elemental realms. These highly ascended beings have an overseer from the twelfth dimension as their inspirer and mentor, helping them stay in the ninth dimension energy. The Salcaritons had mastered incarnation in lower level energy species from the second dimension levels to the fifth. They stopped here, as when a being has reached the fifth level it no longer needs the light soul within, as it has it self become the light creating multidimensional form. They are a wonderful asset to the Intergalactic Council and the experiments.

The Council also expanded the invitation of incarnation to other ethereal beings and highly ascended species, seeking those who could detach from their higher self, enter as a soul, and participate in this new fourth experiment. The Lemurians also decided to continue to incarnate, as by now they had the building blocks within to improve on the learning some of them had failed previously to attain.

After Earth was given time to heal and replenish her lands the new Atlantean society was spread across a large landmass in the warm seas in the southern hemisphere – a green, lush, fertile environment connecting with the sea, with golden sands and fresh land waters. The Council ensured there were the resources to build cities and thrive. The new early Atlanteans built their own cities, travel routes and a temple for their High Light Council. This new Atlantis society had a High Council made up of priests and priestesses with the knowledge needed to support their society. They also had a direct link to the divine source and the Intergalactic Council; with this, they taught the Earth volunteers that came forward for this role about the Law of One. There were also smaller temples, where the new priests and priestesses who volunteered were known as The Ones of the Light. From these beautiful temples they brought physical and mental healing to the Atlantean people, maintaining the high energy needed for the success of the experiment.

For those of you that read this that exist in the lower energy, I should explain how the high ascending beings of the universe think. The Law of One is a spiritual law of the universe that encourages us to accept everyone, everything and ourselves exactly as they are and without judgment. This includes the 'self' and extends to all animals and plants. The Atlanteans were taught that all creatures and beings are learning and evolving, just as the incarnated soul within does. All humans are entitled to their own space, just as the animals are entitled to their own territories. They were taught that they were part of the whole, and every action and thought rippled out across the energy of the universe, which affects everything. For example the higher ascending being can see negative energy and shield themselves from it to keep themselves in pure energy. But lower ascended energy beings cannot see this, and they draw it in, thriving in this energy that causes anger, fear and war with no care for all living things.

In many ascended societies we have connected with, it has been proven that to succeed, the individual understands the Spiritual Law of One; we accept our own divinity, and we begin to listen to our intuition and actively become co-creators in our own lives. The humans were taught to meditate, to keep clarity of mind and their energy levels high, to sustain the connection with the divine high light and love source. We can thank the overseers for spreading this knowledge in seeds of wisdom and teachings throughout the universe.

Towards the end of the first 5,000 years the fourth experiment began to wobble. The same pattern emerged as before, and the Intergalactic Council tried hard to inject love and light into the experiment. They introduced high-energy loving animals from other planets, such as cats, elephants, giraffes and dolphins, and invited further ascended energy beings to reincarnate. This helped for a while but slowly the heavier lower energy again took hold.

At the end of the fourth experiment there was mass destruction as the low energy factions turned against each other in the fight for supremacy. They had developed technology that involved high-energy weapons penetrating deep into the Earth's core. These weapons caused the planet great harm in her core and atmosphere, and this time she reacted by flipping her axis, trying to cleanse herself of the pollution and negative energy. This caused landmasses to move and a mini ice age was created on Earth, and the temperature dropped across sixty percent of its surface, killing plant life and many mammals and humans. Most of the evidence of the fourth Atlantis experiment and previous experiments was destroyed. Surviving humans, mainly in the southern hemispheres, carried on in small pockets of communities. They were now a mixture of original humans, what was left from the three Atlantis experiments, and the fourth Earth experiment. As the planet healed, these humans spread to other areas over time to create small civilisations. The Salcaritons chose to keep incarnating in these Earth humans as a support system, helping to raise the planet's energies in the event of another Atlantis experiment. They tried to guide the people to a simple spiritual existence, respecting animals and Mother Earth as they now called her.

I see from the reports on these four experiments that there was confusion among the Intergalactic Council as to why these experiments kept failing, and what was triggering the humans to sink into lower energies. The master scientists were busy trying to find out what went wrong – was it DNA deterioration, or humans' minds somehow changing frequency, being influenced from some unseen source? The Salcaritons were confused too, as they thought they had mastered this, but some of their incarnated human physical forms also strayed into the lower earth energies. There were many questions that needed answering.

Now, after another day of study, I am back home and I need to clear my mind and evaluate these four experiments before I study the last one, which I am going to be part of.

I have a bit of a treat tonight; I am going with Zogica to a music recital. It's being held in one of our outside recreational meeting spaces, a wonderful, natural place where like-minded ones can gather to enjoy the creativity of their choice. We both love music and the energy it creates. The main instrument is a Zilarian, a row of crystal tubes all set at different energy resonations. The musician gently runs their fingers over this beautiful instrument, using their own vibration, and the instrument sings out its song, which is very hypnotic and relaxing. This is very thoughtful of Zogica, as it will help me switch off and reset my mind energy.

Life Journal – transmission 8 -
'The light within Atlantis'

After my evening off at the music recital I have thrown myself back into my studies. I had a lovely evening with Zogica – whenever we are together my energy feels whole and we have always had a very strong connection with each other. We have known each other since our births, and our parents are great friends. His mother Gilylian is part of the Scared Light Council, which is how they met, and Zogica takes after his father, Pelseti, who is a very creative and intelligent being. We have not talked of bonding yet as we are both so busy with our life paths at the moment, but I do feel in my heart and mind he is the Diacuratian for me. I would like to ask him how deeply he feels before I go into the Sacred Light Temple for the Atlantis mission, as I am not one hundred per cent sure. Although we are telepathic and can read each other's energy auras, we can also protect ourselves from prying minds and keep our true feelings deep inside until we feel it is right to release that energy and share it.

I know there will be a right time for this moment to be presented to me, and I feel our parents waiting in anticipation of a union. Whenever I'm with him and they are around, I see knowing glances of expectancy, which makes me chuckle inside. I'm sure Zogica sees this too, but he has never said anything to me and we respect each other's privacy. I wondered if I should put my personal life and feelings into this part of the journal, but my personal energy is part of my story, and it is my view of the mission ahead. So I guess yes is the answer to that.

In my studies, I have also finally reached the recorded knowledge of the fifth Atlantis experiment. This is a live experiment – taking place on Earth as I record this transmission.

After the ice age was created by the fourth Atlantis experiment, everyone involved thought it best to leave Earth alone for a few thousand years. Eventually the Earth had renewed her energy and cleansed itself, but the ice age did make a lot of mammals extinct and the humans left on the planet survived only in the southern hemisphere where it remained warm. I studied where the first to fourth experiments were held, and with the axis shift this was now in the southern frozen hemisphere and under the ocean and ice. I realised there would be no evidence of these civilisations unless the Earth warmed up in the future, allowing the cold zone to thaw. From my scientific knowledge of observing many planets, this would happen in a time of high population of civilisations that abuse their planets and affect their natural balance. Or it can be an unforeseen event from out of the solar system such as a rogue asteroid or light star changes. Once this warming process is triggered, the beings of the planet cannot reverse it – for example, planet Gaia will always put a stop to her own destruction, and self-cleanse to preserve her survival. Remember, she and other planets are living entities in the second dimensional existence. The Intergalactic Council has observed this many times on other living planets also inhabited by low energy physical beings.

For the fifth Atlantis experiment, the Intergalactic Council decided to try something new. They had had a long time to review the other experiments and draw conclusions about why they had failed.

Before I look fully at the fifth experiment my scientific mind is still trying to digest the reasoning behind the four experiments. The first three experiments lasted a long time, with the control of the Intergalactic Council helping and guiding the experiments. Eventually, the human forms detached from the inner soul link, causing ego behaviour in a lower energy. In all cases, this caused disruption and separation among the humans. This led them to leaving Atlantis and spreading themselves out among the Earth population. This always led to self-destruction among those fighting for power and control, which was the trigger for the end of each experiment. They hoped with the lessons learnt from the returning souls that the next experiment would not fail, but I feel they underestimated the strength of the human essence, self-will leading to an egocentric existence. I have to admit I felt it was as if the Intergalactic Council was trying to tame the human form, keeping it as a shell simply to serve the purpose of the divine source and gain knowledge. But the lesson learnt is if you create a species it will eventually develop and find its own way of being. They will be influenced by the world around them and create their own identity and reality.

I could see that starting off with a high energy DNA human form with one gender, who understands it is here to serve the whole, is a safe concept for success. But as you have seen, time caused the human form to change and grow its own individual identity. The freedom of choice was always there and could have gone two ways. They could either understand and ascend as the individual with the soul back to the ethereal being they were, or find a lower, dark energy of greed and self to exist in, not acknowledging the higher energy soul and divine energy. What is clear is that this darker, lower energy is so heavy; they are swamped by it and cannot see the pure light energy.

There was some confusion on how the latter happened. This was because when the first experiment was held, Earth was a high pure energy planet. There were some lower energy beings on the planet, but they were focused on eating, keeping warm and surviving day-to-day, and they did not hunt each other. If anything, they worked in small communities to help each other. So where did such a lower vibration energy come from? There was only one solution I could see in the records of knowledge. The master scientists suggested that when the higher ascended human form disconnected from the high love light source, it hit rock bottom, plunged into a lower energy field and suffered from shock, as it had to adapt to this new lower energy. The behaviour of the human became erratic, triggering the egotistic dominancy survival behaviour. With this imbalance, their energies could not flow normally, causing physical disease and mental illness.

I will have a bit more time soon to tell you about the fifth Atlantis experiment, but now it's time to take Dolso to the outside recreational space for some fun. He loves to run and blunder around and is always the centre of attention when he meets my friends.

Life Journal – transmission 9 -
'The light within Atlantis'

I am still hard at work in the Sacred Light Temple tucked away in my study chamber, but thought I would take a little break to update my journal. This is all so fascinating for me, this big learning journey I am on. I am coming to the end of this study period and I estimate a couple more sessions before I meet with my mission team again for the next stage.

Here is some knowledge for you of what I have learnt. After the four failed Atlantis experiments, the overseers and Intergalactic Council chose to have one final go. They decided to populate Atlantis with new humanoid forms of genders, male and female, but chose to change their DNA.

They asked the Salcaritons to review the DNA, and their findings showed that when linked with the chakras, it was too weak in frequency to maintain the fifth dimensional link. The DNA needed to be structured to support a strong link with a self-adjusting frequency to maintain balance. With their knowledge of studying many species in the universe, they adjusted the new human DNA to a twelve helix DNA that had previously worked well in other situations. This was a high frequency system that would stay activated while the physical human was connected to the divine light source. With the 12 chakras and this high frequency DNA, the Atlanteans were able to live in a five dimensional status within the Earth's energy. With this unified combination of DNA and chakras they were psychic, with clairsentience, clairaudience and clairvoyance abilities. This enabled telekinesis, which powered them to use their minds to manifest material substance and manipulate it by drawing on the high consciousness cosmic matrix. They were the most physically powerful of all the humanoids yet developed.

The humanoid form would have to work to maintain this frequency of connection by meditation, self-healing and being as one in the unconditional love frequency. If there was another failure, the DNA would start to shut down and could convert back to the two-stranded DNA of the lower energy humanoids. This is seen in many lower energy beings descendants who are the result of other star being visits to Earth before the Atlantis experiments. The Salcaritons designed this new DNA so that humans who inherited it could, if fallen into the lower energies, be reactivated when the time was right. They would be reconnecting with the belief system of the divine unconditional light source from the twelfth dimension. The Intergalactic Council was making sure that if they chose to continue with Earth as a base experiment and library of information, they could draw on this built-in safety mechanism for the future of humans.

Up to this point they had been recreating the human species, but now they decided that if the fifth experiment failed, they would let the Atlantean humans that choose to stay, spread around Earth and live their lives, watching how new societies developed. So they were already planning a sixth experiment as a fall-back. The Salcaritons would oversee this sixth experiment and be the main incarnated souls among the humans. They would also carefully select other high status beings to incarnate. This would depend on how the Earth progressed, and whether it would need redirection towards the unconditional love energy source.

They also built into their high frequency DNA the knowledge

and instincts about survival, how to build their own homes and Temples through mind materialisation, and how to live on Earth's land. They made Earth part of their energy connection as well as staying connected to the higher energy light source of the divine. They created a beautiful race of people, tall with blond silver hair, blue eyes, olive skin, and great clear-seeing intelligence. Built into the DNA were variants such as hair and eye colour that would show in future generations, creating a race of individuals. The humanoid form would also maintain the telepathic abilities and telekinesis, while some would also have teleporting skills.

As there were more primitive humans on the planet who survived the mini ice age, some of these were descendants of survivors from the previous experiments who were living in small communities. Because of their isolation, they had learned to live peacefully, helped by the influence of the Salcaritons' incarnations, which had continued throughout this interesting phase of Earth's climate adjustment as she renewed and cleansed herself.

I feel that out of chaos came a form of ascension among the more primitive human survivors. Even though they had achieved this, they did not want the lower energy beings affecting the new Atlantean human energies. The ascended scientists suspected that the old human DNA was tainted and had not yet finally concluded why four experiments had ultimately failed. They decided not to interfere with the Earth's old inhabitants at this stage of the experiment and let them progress naturally, observing them as a side experiment with the support of the Salcaritons.

The decision regarding where to base the new Atlantis was

based on how the Earth was healing after the mini ice age, since the landmasses in some northern areas were still settling and regenerating. Because of this, they decided that the main Atlantis city would be sited on a large, separate landmass, which was again in the warm southern hemisphere. This was now a stable environment, and only future positive energy growth was foreseen. The master scientists made sure the chosen lands had what was needed to build Temples and homes, with a sustainable supply of food and fresh water. Following advice from the Salcaritons, they decided that the temples should be built over the energy lines that run through and round the Earth, so they could tap in to the planet's power. This would connect the physical beings to Earth's pure energy and help keep the planet balanced. It would also help the Earth chakra energy to give grounding strength, helping to balance the multidimensional energies.

The Temples were pyramids of sacred geometry and stunning architecture, many of them covered in a dome of projected crystalline amplified energy light that looked like a glowing force field. The energy fields projected above the Temples were of various colours, according to the purpose of the them, and glowed day and night like the Aurora seen on Earth.

The main city of Atlantis had an Earth measurement of fourteen miles at the time of this transmission. The city was designed with the Temple of light in the centre, elevated above the land on high ground. The high status families – the ascended teaching masters, priests and priestesses – lived in homes in the shadow of the Temple, while the rest of the population spread out around it. Rings of waterways and gardens expanded outwards from the Temple creating an island effect, and as the city grew over time, they made sure everyone relaxed within a tranquil atmosphere. Away from the main city, eleven further cities were placed on Earth, also with Temples, which were individually connected to the Twelve Spiritual Universal Laws. Each city was placed away from the lower energy human populations. Each of the city Temples had a high ranking light being called a Celestial Guardian, ensuring the Atlantean people did not lose sight of their spiritual mission while on Earth. The Temples varied in appearance, all reflecting the pyramid style but with their own uniqueness. As well as being built over the energy lines, they were also placed near water, by the ocean, lakes or rivers, because the energy of flowing water helps with healing and allows access for travel. The Intergalactic Council also decided to create an Earth bio shield – a protective energy shield designed to keep the climate at an even temperature, and protect the Atlantean cities from the harsher elements of Earth.

The Twelve Spiritual Universal Laws mentioned above will add to your understanding of my future mission, so I'll share them with you now.

1. The law of oneness: Everyone is part of the whole universe energy consciousness and the matrix of each dimensional layer. Every action you take affects everything throughout the universe. Just imagine everything continually moves, flows and vibrates with energy, and never stops. Your mood and thoughts affect your own energy and vibration, which shimmers out on a wave of energy, bumping and docking into other energy vibrations. A way to simply describe this is to imagine a pool of calm water; when you throw a small object into the pool, its impact causes the water to ripple outwards. It starts with close and strong ripples at the centre of impact, gradually becoming further apart as the waves travel. The ripple then hits a rock and disperses, going on and on and affecting everything in its path.

2. The law of vibration: All that exists is energy with a vibration frequency. The level of this vibration varies according to the dimensional levels each being or object exists in. To maintain the best vibration for the individual, you need to attune to Nature's vibration and observe. On Earth, for example, observing a bee pollinating a plant creates a meditative state for the watcher. It would attune the human being to Nature's vibration and frequency, calibrating their own to the balanced, enlightened state of the bee's energy frequency. When this is achieved and you are fully in tune with the bee, you can communicate with it, as you can with all things plant and animal.

3. The law of relativity: This law reminds physical beings of consciousness, explaining how to remain connected to their heart consciousness by loving all in their world and beyond. We are all taught this on an emotional and spiritual level, embodying the thought of transition from physical being to living in non-physical multidimensional existence. When we link our thoughts through Nature's energy and loving the natural world, it enhances our own reality. To stay in the higher divine energy is to stop the lower energies controlling your reality, so existence through high unconditional love conscious being is crucial.

4. The law of rhythm: This law reflects the rhythm of energy's that flow through sound and light. It embraces the flow of, for example, a planet's energies, the rhythm of the planet's flow from day to night, and the growth of the planet's evolution. Thinking in the positive light ensures a smooth rhythm of existence. This starts within the physical nucleolus all the way to the light divine energy of source in the twelfth dimension. The flow of smooth rhythm is key to all being in balance. If this flow is not in rhythm, it affects the beings' connection with the divine, and their journey of ascension can be halted until the smooth rhythm returns.

5. The law of polarity: This law illustrates there is always an opposite of what you see or feel. For example, the planetary forces that exist in the first dimensions, or at the north and south poles, where an unseen magnetic force holds them in place. This leads me to the mind; if you find yourself in a challenging situation, you turn your mind to the opposite feeling, for example negative to positive. You can then shift your own energy from one to the other, which helps you stay balanced in the light energy nearer to source.

6. The law of action: Your actions come from thought, movement and voice. This law is to remind us that there are consequences from actions that the individual chooses to take. Unconditional love is a pure energy that brings forgiveness, eliminates karma and brings the highest blessing from the divine source. Living in this energy creates compassion and empathy; this changes the energy around you, creating great possibilities through positive thoughts and actions. The energy needed to make profound judgements before you take action can be created from sound through chant, speaking prayer and song. This practice helps the mind remain aware of this law, and attunes it to the manifestation of the positive energy for true thoughts and actions.

7. The law of attraction: This encourages you to take

ownership of your existence through thoughts and actions, and helps you to draw the creation of choice into existence. It should always be in the positive way of thinking to keep you in the higher energies. As soon as you start to lay blame at another being's feet for your own mistakes, you create negative thoughts which draw in the lower energies. When you understand the spiritual law of attraction, you no longer lay blame on anyone else or project your judgements and feelings onto others. You live in the belief of the source of unconditional love.

8. The law of manifestation: When you remember to act within the boundary of love, that's what you attract. Act in the boundaries of hate and – you guessed it – that is what comes back. Every being has the power that creates what is in their lives. You can all live comfortable, happy lives, deserving this and working for the good of all instead of self. Your attitude and thought creates who you are and the reality around you. Imagine the worlds where they all work in harmony; everyone has food, shelter, love and kindness, creating daily miracles of wonder. All work in the positive energies that attract back to each and every one. This was witnessed in the early stages of all the Atlantis experiments.

9. The law of karma: Because there is a spiritual balance for all, every being has a responsibility to keep this divine balance. Remember the ripple effect in the law of one – these energies ripple out and you draw back the type of energy you are sending. Good intent and good deeds contribute to good karma and future happiness, while bad intent and bad deeds contribute to bad karma and future suffering. In the early stages of all the Atlantean experiments there was no karma, due to the high ascended energy working for the whole not the one. Then, as the human essence developed ego and self-importance, the energy started to get lower, drawing negative, dense energy back to them. The karma energy became part of their day-to-day lives.

10. The law of transmutation: Put simply, if you live your life in unconditional love, you can transform it. You will live with no harmful emotional attachments that could create the lower heavy energies for you or others. You are then free from any boundaries of restriction and can fulfill your potential. You will be released from the restriction of the lower energy that attracts hate and draw in the light energy, so you know only happiness. This is achieved with positive processing of your thoughts through meditation and healing; if you support each other in creating good for all, there are no bad feelings.

11. The law of gender: Since the start of creation, all beings have had both male and female energies. Throughout the cosmos, there are species with individual gender and species with no gender. Both need to find the feminine and masculine balance to achieve oneness with themselves, which brings the connection to working as a whole for the good of all.

12. The law of intention: When you reach the divine moment of full clarity in unconditional love, you can ask the universe to assist you in all things. You will carry on ascending for the good of the whole not the one. Everything you do is powered by your intentions. If you wish for the highest ideal of peace, but inside you don't really think this is achievable, it will not be created. The intention of doubt will then override the original first thought of peace. If you really believe there can be peace then that is what will be created, with the positive inner intention of belief.

I guess you are starting to see a pattern here, that the higher pure unconditional love energy creates a better existence for all. These universal laws are also what were given to our world many hyons ago and working with them, we have adapted and changed towards the fifth dimensional energy.

To return to Atlantis, the way the experiment worked had been altered, and in the first phase of the fifth experiment, the Intergalactic Council did not supply the materials for the building of the cities. The humans learned to pull together to build their homes and cities, using Earth's natural resources and the materialisation gift creating what else was needed to aid this. The master scientists made sure the landmasses they inhabited provided all they needed. Their water came from fresh water wells in each city, and there were central lakes and bathing areas for communities to enjoy. They also loved gardens, waterfalls and fountains as this energy provided a peaceful spiritual area for recharging.

The evidence shows this was successful, as they helped build each other's homes and worked for the whole not for the one, which kept them in the high frequency energy. In the beginning, it was an existence of simplicity, maintaining the divine connection and making sure all needs were met in the love and light energy. As time went on the inhabitants built more refined homes, using gold, bronze, copper and gems for internal and exterior decoration. The social structure became more civilised and they managed to retain their elevated energy connection needed for the experiment not to fail. The arts like painting and music prevailed, with buildings dedicated to these pursuits. The children were nurtured so they could be the best they could, finding their true life path amongst their people.

An interesting piece of information is that in the other four experiments, the humans' incarnated souls all knew each other before they incarnated. The Intergalactic Council had set up a school of experiment called The School of Light, where all chosen beings could gather to learn about the new human form and what they could expect when they incarnated. Each time a new generation was needed, the selected beings would familiarise themselves with each other at The School of Light before incarnating into the Atlanteans. In the fourth experiment, they even chose their bonding mates before they came to Earth.

They then chose to close the school for the fifth experiment and they did not meet any other beings before incarnating. This was on the recommendation of the Salcaritons, who felt the Intergalactic Council should properly challenge this experiment to get the fullest information from the results, and hopefully giving answers to why parts were successful and past experiments eventually failed. Individually, the beings to incarnate were familiarised with the human form on their home planet or realm, with members of the Intergalactic Council helping with this, as I will be. They really wanted to test the waters this time and felt confident that with the Salcaritons' newfound science on incarnation, they could afford to introduce more change to the boundaries of the experiment.

When the fifth Atlantis experiment was created, the Intergalactic Council decided to house twelve cosmic beings from the tenth dimension, in a star ship held above the centre of the city in Earth's atmosphere. These were highly evolved light beings all connected with the various home planets and realms of those who were incarnating. The star ship was designed to be a Temple of Light of unconditional love for teaching and knowledge for the Atlantean people. These twelve cosmic beings are called the Celestial Guardians and their role is to oversee the experiment then report back to the Intergalactic Council and the overseers. The star ship also has another vital role; it has a calentian crystal that powers the Earth's biosphere dome. It is also a computer that records everything that has happened, like a library of knowledge on Atlantis and its history. The Temple of Light in central Atlantis had a smaller calentian crystal that connected with the higher star ship crystal. The other eleven Temples in the other cities also had crystals that all interlinked with the main Atlantean Light Temple crystal and the star ship.

The human population has chosen priests and priestesses to lead the people in the Twelve Laws, and carry out healing among them. The twelve Celestial Guardians only connect to these chosen humans, and have no contact with others on Earth. Their purpose is to help the experiment keep its energies on the high frequency required for success.

As time progressed with the fifth experiment, the Atlantean people developed a hierarchy of rule, part of which includes a highly ascended family to oversee each city, working as part of the Light Temple. You would understand this as a kind of royal family ruling the lands. This family was also given access to the twelve Celestial Guardians.

Well that's it for this light day, the transmission took longer than expected, my mind is tired and I am now going to rest with my family and Dolso. I will be studying for next couple of days, and then I will add more to my journal.

Life Journal – transmission 10 -
'The light within Atlantis'

I have now finished my phase of study and Telcarian has suggested I take a couple of light days to myself before we start the next phase of the mission. I have to admit I agree with him, as it is nice sometimes to have a change of scenery before you let your mind become busy again.

Last night, I made plans with Zogica for us to go to a range of mountains called Alcerian Touliza, which means Crystal Light. My parents visit them often and named me after them as they saw me as a precious being, the light in their hearts, and wanted to show their love for me in my name.

On this light day of our trip, I woke to see the amazing phenomenon of auras and colour clouds we call Zelicann had cleared, and the beautiful light star is back in our skies. I would have usually been aware of its progress in the course of my science studies, but have been so busy at the Temple I forgot to check.

The mountains are beautiful, full of pure energy and a very spiritual place to visit and reflect on life, our world and much more. When the energies are right at certain times of the year, the mountains give us a light show. The crystal formations release the energy that has been absorbed from the light star and it appears as pulsating coloured light beams travelling up to the stars. This is a magical experience to encounter and I have witnessed it once as child when my parents took me there. We will miss it this time around, but I plan to go back so I can have that experience again with Zogica.

We left home early as the light star rays came up over the

horizon, and the moons were still in view in the dawn sky. As we travelled in our craft, we sat and enjoyed the views, plains of grassland, and areas of denser plants that covered the landscape. Some of the landscape can be quite rugged, but there are lush areas with lakes and beautiful waterfalls along the way. I always admire the nature on our planet, the beautiful flying creatures and the spiritual land creatures. My favourite is the winged four-legged mammal similar to an Earth horse. Like all creatures, it has adapted to our planet's weather pattern, sheltering in the days of the Zelicann. It runs the plains of our planet, and flies to greet us when we come to the surface to live and explore.

Our animals are not what some beings would call pets or food for us; they are all free to live in the balance of nature. Even though Dolso was given to me as a gift, he is still a free spirit; but we are so bonded he chooses to stay with me in free will. If he ever wanted to go I would have to respect his decision. This actually reminds me of the cats I read about, that were brought to the Atlantis experiments to raise the energies. They would select their physical being, or they would choose to live in the wild nature of Earth.

We find the animals on our planet are very high-energy beings; the first and second dimensional life forms have adapted to the higher five dimensional energy the planet now contains. There is no food chain in the animal hierarchy and like us, they eat plant life, so they can live without fear of the threat of attack. This brings a natural harmony and helps with the overall energy balance of our planet. Many, many hyons ago this was a different story, but we have ascended now to respect all life, with its different intelligences and energy frequencies – all the animals and insects of our world have evolved with us in the ascension energies. Their consciousness is also expanding and we are fortunate to be able to connect to all these and understand the meaning of divine creation – for the whole not the one.

The Zelicann can occur anywhere on the planet. It is full of energy that sends flashes of energised light to the land. The animals have adapted like us, so they, too, can sense its arrival, and the flying species know to leave the area it will affect. Silence can befall the land, a true sign of Zelicann's arrival, but we do not fear it – we have learnt to embrace this energy, and have crystal technology that enables us to harness its power for our domed cities.

Diacurat is also what I would describe as a water planet, with surface oceans as well as underground ones. Our above-ground landmass covers about 65 percent of the planet. The oceans below have formed in huge underground open spaces; many thousands of hyons ago, these helped us develop ways of living underground as well as on the surface. The rock formation of our planet is a crystalline structure, varying from very hard rocks like the Earth diamond to softer formations. It has a fluorescence about it in places that gives light in the underground oceans. The life these underground oceans hold is different to that of the upper oceans – a never-ending source of fascination.

We arrived at the mountains as the light starlight was at its strongest, and found a suitable place to land and set up our camp. We chose an area of the mountains with a beautiful lake, a waterfall, shade and easy access to the sights we sought. The area we were in has a lovely temperate climate, although our planet does have colder spots on the axial points, similar to but not as extreme as those on Earth. As we are in our dry season, we decided to rest in the open under the clear skies, moons and stars. After making a meal, we spent the evening talking about many things of interest to us and reflecting on our lives. I also updated Zogica on my studies so far, as he was fascinated by what I could reveal to him. Then we spent a long time staring at the stars, listening to the song of Nature that was all around us, and embracing the energy.

Then it happened – we were holding hands and no words or thoughts of our love connection were needed; we both just knew. We were so connected we both simultaneously let our multidimensional body disconnect from our physical body and we floated up. I was a bit wary, as I know Zogica was not used to multidimensional travel, but my energy helped to sustain us both. In this state, we only have mind-to-mind communication, so we connected our energy and started travelling across the mountains, swooping up and down into the valleys, exploring them as we went. Then we dropped into the huge lake by our camp; this was just amazing as we travelled under the surface through the clear water, seeing clearly the creatures that live there. I was in awe of the fish that can fly; they have multi-coloured bodies that pulsate with energy and are fascinating to watch. There are also fish that glow with energy, lighting up the waters at night. It was all so beautiful, as if we had our own underwater special nature light show to observe.

For the first time in my life, I felt fully attuned to our planet and the universe beyond. Eventually we returned back to our physical form, digesting our unique experience; Zogica was in awe at what had just happened to him. He felt that something inside him had awoken, connecting him to the world around him and bringing a clarity of existence. We chatted for a while about our experience and then fell asleep under the stars in a wonderful state of euphoria.

Life Journal – transmission 11 -
'The light within Atlantis'

My last transmission about our trip was interrupted, as Telcarian called to see me and after that, I needed my rest. To finish my story: The next light day we woke early just as the light star rays rose up to light up our world. We watched the light climb up the mountainside; as this happened the rock crystals changed colours and sparkled with colours of purple, lilac and blue mixed with silvers and the white of the mountain. As the rays hit the crystals, they absorb the light and reflect their colours back into our world – it is a spectacular sight to behold. It's at moments like this that I realise what a beautiful planet we have.

I now felt very rested and attuned to everything around me. Our out of body experience was still with us in mind and heart, and had brought us closer together. The scientist in me feels I should explain how the out of body experience could happen.

Many thousands of hyons ago we were lower energy beings, existing in a lower energy state of mind and body, similar to the Earth I have been telling you about. Over hyons, we started to realise that if we did not connect to our planet and its life source we would perish through self-destruction. We did not have highly ascended incarnated souls to help us with this; we came to this understanding because the overseers chose to visit us and give us our life light crystal. As you can imagine, this was a time of great change for our planet. There were ones among us who feared the beings of love at the start, but time soon healed that fear and helped us progress into the light energy.

The crystal contained great knowledge and ascension lessons to help guide us on this journey of enlightenment. When the overseers came they looked among our people and selected twelve to head up the Sacred Light Temple, and helped us build the Temple to house the crystal. They taught us the laws they live by and watched us from afar, as they still do today. Were we another experiment? I would say now we were, but what defines an experiment? To me, an experiment is conducted to make a discovery, test a hypothesis, or demonstrate a known fact. I will let you decide.

The overseers came to us at a time when our society had already started to ascend, many not wanting the negative existence we were living in anymore. The overseers saw hope in our planet, having watched us from the tenth to twelve dimensions, and knowing when to approach a planet or civilisation to help bring its beings into the light.

Over many, many hyons we slowly ascended into the five dimensional energy ways of being and starting to vibrate in pure unconscious love energy. We achieved this through meditation and mindfulness and with this mind change, our body form has changed too. Our physical body now self-heals and we have no disease among us. Our telepathic minds can attune to frequencies of all consciousness energy and we have learned connect to lower energy consciousness, for example with crystals or animals. We can attune to their frequencies and ask them to aid us (remember the crystal flying craft I mentioned earlier). We have now found multidimensional consciousness, which has enabled us to form an ethereal body that sits within our physical body parameters. While this multidimensional body sits within, it is also held by an outer energy field some would know as an aura. Having a multidimensional body means we can adapt to various dimension frequencies – at the moment, our ability is one to six. Some of us have learnt though thought to detach ourselves from the physical body and live outside it. I have managed to do this for a while now, but I still need to break away from my doubts to completely achieve full out of body consciousness for longer periods.

The multidimensional body does not need food nourishment, it survives on the high energy vibration of pure love, a fuel that is unseen but felt all around us when you are open to it, as a high frequency energy vibrating in harmonic sound and light waves.

When I was out of the physical body with Zogica, I felt we could have gone on forever, gone anywhere in the universe and done anything, as there is no doubt in my mind and heart when I am with him. This experience connected us in a new way and we now know we are partners for life, although he understands I have this Atlantis journey to take before we can properly bond. Bonding to us is a life commitment as partners and mates, which is celebrated in a ceremony with our family, friends and witnesses. As a species, we still produce our young through physical contact; we want younglings, but this will be further on in our future. We have many hyons ahead of us to make these plans and it is key for our future that we all travel our true path for the whole. Of course it is not all about me; Zogica is excelling in his design and technology work in the architectural building field. This is going to take him to other worlds where he can learn from other beings and bring this knowledge back to Diacurat. The plan at the moment is he will do this over the time I am at the Temple, keeping in touch by mind and vision screens when we can.

Life Journal – transmission 12 –
'The light within Atlantis'

We returned from our trip both felling refreshed and excited by our separate and joint futures. We were laughing on the way back, discussing whether or not to tell our parents. But we knew we had to, as mine would know straight away that something was different. I could feel my energy was altered and uplifted – when we recognise the stronger love for a fellow being it is hard to hide that spark of pure love energy.

My parents were out on my return, so we decided to ask both sets of parents to gather in the evening at our resting chambers for an evening of enlightenment! You can imagine their reaction when we told them – they were overjoyed that we had committed to each other. I know Zogica's mother Antoglia wanted the bonding ceremony before I committed fully to the Atlantis mission and my time in the Temple. But we explained how we plan to use the time apart for further development, even though it will be in different ways. The trouble was, I did not know yet how the mission would go, or what was planned for me, so I asked them all to have faith in the path of light, and trust all would be well.

You can see the little bit of doubt we still have in us showed in this experience with Antoglia, who wanted us to bond straight away. This was because she was worried something would change our minds, as she loves us both so much. I can easily see the difference between her and my parents, who, with their more highly ascended minds, had no doubt, just acceptance of the now. This does not make them better or worse than Antoglia, but shows the path we need to take to ascend beyond these feelings. Feelings of doubt block our energy paths and are the last negative energies from our third dimensional existence. The lesson is to trust the journey for the good of the whole, knowing when the time is right we will be joined together if this is our destiny.

As I lie here with Dolso, reflecting on the last two days, I feel so rested and focused. I do believe that by the way he's lying across me, fast asleep, he has missed me. I am thinking about what's to come, but a lot of it is still guesswork. Tomorrow, I am off to the Temple to meet with Telcarian and Ioliismiem to plan the next stage of our mission to Atlantis.

Life Journal – transmission 13 –
'The light within Atlantis'

I travelled this light day to the Sacred Light Temple with my parents, as they also go there to carry out their light work roles. I have already told you about my father Holhfen's work, but I have yet to tell you about my mother's. She is best described as a senior member of the Council, of high priestess status. In some civilisations in the universe, a priestess is a pure divine being in body and soul, who never mates or has a life partner. This is seen more in the lower energy beings, so the priests and priestess's energy can stay pure for the divine connection; this used to be our way too. But since we have ascended into the fifth dimensional energy, we can now live with a bonded partner and carry out this high status energy work in a Temple. When necessary, our emotions are contained, physically and mentally, and do not affect our clarity of mind as it did thousands of hyons ago.

One of my mother's roles is working with the healing multidimensional energies, and teaching these skills to others. She can take on multidimensional form, leave her physical body and can travel for long periods - to similar star beings' home planets, and realms through dimensions and light way portals. She is from a long line of ascended masters who have defined this energy travel – this will also be my future role in our society.

I had a wonderful light day at the Temple and the mission plans are now set. When I got there, Telcarian and Ioliismiem led me to another chamber that was new to me. It was beautifully decorated with cut crystals and wall art reflecting our planet's history. The light in there changed softly to different colours and was very calming. I learned that this is a meditating and rest area; there was floor seating and places to lie down. There was also a light dream machine from Telcarian's home world given as a gift. This could take you into a dream state where you could create a reality and act out scenarios of your choice, which could be recorded to return to in the future. I found it all very fascinating and look forward to trying it out some light day.

I was introduced to Avielil from the realm Salcariton. I mentioned these beautiful beings earlier in my journal. Their form is unconditional love and light with a violet shimmering colour, but when they choose to work with us or at other energy levels lower than theirs, they take on a physical form. They have no gender, pale violet pulsating skin, a head and limbs, and only telepathic communication. They move with such grace that I was in awe of his divine presence. Avielil had joined us to help with the stage when I split my multidimensional self. He told me he wanted to be part of this mission from the beginning to the end, to help us succeed and learn all we can from the experience.

Telcarian and Ioliismiem both explained the next stage of my preparation for this mission to Atlantis was to perfect my multidimensional separation. Ioliismiem explained that as we still have a physical shell, our multidimensional body stays attached to this for our life link on Diacurat. On our physical death, our multidimensional being will be fully free and will ascend into the higher energy planes, as it is called back to the tenth to twelfth dimensional realms and the overseers. There, we have an existence linking up with other beings gone before us from our planet. Because of this physical link I need to perfect this transition, so that when I split my multidimensional form I have the energy and mind strength to sustain it for the time period needed, keeping my physical form alive.

I will be multidimensional travelling with Telcarian and Ioliismiem, which means I will be in good hands, as this is something their species mastered a long time ago. They will take me on journeys to their home planets and through light way portals to other planets and realms. At all times I will stay connected to my physical body shell. At first I will be placed in a life pod to monitor my vital signs and strength of connection. They will build up the moments of travel away from my physical body and my ability to stay connected. When I have stabilised the energy build-up needed, we will then be ready for the multidimensional split before I start my mission to Atlantis as an incarnated soul.

This will need daily commitment so the time has come to move into the Temple, where I can be fully focused on the tasks ahead of me. Over the next couple of days I will be sorting out my belongings and moving; the prospect of the adventures ahead of me fills me with excitement!

Life Journal – transmission 14 -
'The light within Atlantis'

I am now living here in the Temple and have settled into my chambers. They are very relaxing and I am sitting here watching Dolso play, so I have some time to update my journal. I have a lovely living and resting area that opens out on to a beautiful garden and space for Dolso, the living space has crystal walls and decoration that reflects our nature – a very calming space. I have my crystal communication screen to contact my friends and keep up to date with the world around me. I cannot divulge what I am doing so my communications are social. I have an eating space but my nourishment meals are with other Temple members or sometimes alone, depending on what's going on.

Dolso has settled in and my parents visit us when they can so he has the family bond needed. I know others will fall in love with him too, so his spiritual love needs will be met.

The Temple is a huge complex. The main Sacred Light Temple is above ground level under a bio dome, and then layers of the pyramid-shaped building spread out from the surface level to underground levels, all with different purposes. The main meeting areas are on the higher levels, including the big chamber for high status gatherings, then there are the healing meditation areas, the science development mind areas, living areas – and amongst all this are terraces, courtyards and gardens. I have memorised the path map to find my way around, and can use the teleportation points too for the main areas of the Temple if I choose. I guess I can also be multidimensional when I'm travelling around.

Later this light day, I am off to see the multidimensional observation chamber they have set up for me and to gain more understanding of what's involved.

Life Journal – transmission 15 -
'The light within Atlantis'

The multidimensional chamber that holds my observation pod was larger than I expected, with a central area where my pod stands and crystal technology to record everything. The pod had a clear energy cover that moves over me and gently rotates to monitor my physical form. Around this were other beds for those joining me in multidimensional travelling.

Above this space was an elevated viewing platform where others could come and view progress. The elected viewers included those from our own Temple, plus invited off-world beings. I had not realised I was going to be of such interest and monitored this way! But then again I am not surprised as it is of great scientific and spiritual interest to many. There was also a large crystal screen for observing our journeys and destinations, which Telcarian and Ioliismiem will be mind-teleporting to the chamber at a pre-selected light-sound frequency. The master scientists will monitor our progress, reporting this back to the Intergalactic Council.

This light day, I tried out the observation pod with great curiosity. I wore light clothing and had to ensure I had had enough food and liquid to sustain me before I entered. I lay down and when the clear energy cover came over and started to gently rotate, I was instructed to close my eyes as if I was going into a meditative state. They asked me, when I was ready, to separate myself into multidimensional energy, but I found it difficult to achieve. I realised I usually did this when I was relaxed, and not under pressure with lots of eyes on me. Ioliismiem reminded me to imagine I was somewhere I love to be, and breathe in the memory of that place to help me relax. I took myself back to the Alcerian Touliza Mountains and the moment when Zogica and myself multidimensional body travelled. This did the trick – the next thing I knew, I had detached from my physical form and was up on the observation platform looking down on myself.

It is important I do this with someone experienced first, as our plan to leave the planet and travel the universe means encountering layers of energies, dimensions and unseen energy forces. You can get into trouble if you do not know the maps for multidimensional travel. Part of this learning will be downloading to my memory the maps where I can travel. It is important I stick to them – they have been used for many hyons to keep us clear of lower energies in the universes that can harm our energies or draw us into unforeseen dimensional holes. We could get confused and lost, which could break our link with our physical self. But on the positive side, I am safe if I follow all the instructions my teachers give me.

I am back in my resting chamber now, enjoying some Dolso and me time while I update my journal. I feel quite exhilarated by this light day's multidimensional travel attempts. The feedback was positive and they were pleased with my progress. I am looking forward to contacting Zogica later to see what his plans are and how he is.

Life Journal – transmission 16 -
'The light within Atlantis'

On reflection, we all felt yesterday went really well and tomorrow, I am starting a regime of forty light days of practicing multidimensional travelling. Meanwhile, I will reflect on my conversation with Zogica before I go. We are missing each other so we are going to communicate as often as we can, so that our energies are not affected by our separation. We were joking around and said separation can make the love bond grow stronger, but on reflection I think we are right, as it is a test of the bond connection we have declared for each other. He is doing really well and has been designing a creative centre for the arts of our people. This is a big honour for him and shows his father's trust in his skills. He wants it to be a combination of clear structure and solid form, linking with beautiful outside landscaping. The creative arts will be viewed inside and out, and he is also exploring the idea of an outdoor amphitheatre. It sounds wonderful and he hopes to show me some drawings soon for my approval!

He is also going to take some tuition from my mother on multidimensional travelling to help him grow his consciousness boundaries while I am in the Temple. This means that when we can be together again permanently, he is not left behind in my energy ascension levels and we can multidimensional travel together beyond our planet.

Life Journal – transmission 17 -
'The light within Atlantis'

We have now completed three local multidimensional travels; Telcarian took me through a light way portal yesterday to another planet, which was a magical experience for me. I will reveal some of the places I have visited when I can so you can be part of my wonderful journey. I will keep my descriptions brief, as most of you will be able to look up the universal knowledge library to find out more about the places we visit if they interest you. If you are reading these transmissions in written form on a third dimension energy world, I hope what I describe is translated well so it will ignite your imaginations as you visualise the wonder of these places.

The first planet we visited is called Castrolian and is far away from my solar system, which is why we travelled through a light way portal. The planet is one of the places where the Salcaritons have chosen to incarnate. This was my first light way portal experience; I would describe it as a portal transporter tunnel through the universe created by light, harmonic sound, dimensional energy and frequency light vibration. A single physical or multidimensional form, up to the size of a large star ship, can travel through these light way portals. There are thousands of them all mapped out for our use in the universe; if we discover a new destination, a new one is created for this type of travel. There are also light star gate stations through the universe that can be resting points or meeting places for beings who want to travel together, or for intergalactic forces organising events in the universe.

I tell you it was not what I expected. I thought I would get the sensation of whizzing through a swirling tunnel of energy and popping out the other end. Instead, I experienced a telepathic thought connecting to the light way portal frequency. Every light way portal has its own frequency setting and your own individual frequency is added to the network. When you connect to the frequency you set your intent – the destination – and ask to be accepted into the light way portal for your journey. Then I was suddenly there, in the blink of an eye! The light way portal connected with my frequency as well transporting me safely. You can only travel this way with permission from the Intergalactic Council, and when your frequency has been entered into the light star stations at the star gates. This is to stop any misuse of them by lower energy star beings who would not have good intentions for the whole. To stay connected to my physical body in the observation chamber, the intent is set to stay linked. The power of this thought alone links you to the threads of life. Imagine infinite silver threads connecting you to your physical life form, travelling any distance across the universe, and your life force keeping you linked at all times.

We did not show ourselves to the Castrolian people on our journey, and we travelled the planet unseen, observing as we went. We can cloak our energies to the species of the planet, and if it lies in a third to fourth dimensional energy, they would not be able to see our higher light energy forms. In the case of the Castrolians, they are now ascending and aware of the Salcaritons and the existence of other species. But it's best not to upset this balance until the Salcaritons and Intergalactic Council advise us that the Castrolians are ready to see other species.

Castrolian is one of twelve main planets within the Castrolian solar system, orbiting their light star, which is larger than ours.

The planet that contains life is smaller than Diacurat and orbits a larger planet. I think this larger planet bears the closest resemblance to Earth's solar system planet with rings in its appearance, and there are also a couple of moons orbiting Castrolian. Castrolian has some similarities to Earth and my planet; it has a liquid substance that helps to sustain life, as water does on Earth and Diacurat, but the make-up of the liquid is chemically different and is a life source produced from inside the planet. The planet is inhabited by plant life, animals and physical energy beings. Its history of existence is all very similar to our planet's timeline and solar system.

The Castrolian civilisation supports beings that are very ethereal in nature. Think of the elemental beings existing in the universe that live in the kingdoms of Salcariton, who are small magical creatures in human form, but with pointed ears and fine facial features. The Castrolians protect their planet and live in what you would understand as a loving, supportive and kind way. They do not hurt each other and there is no hate or anger amongst them, but like the lower energy humans, they have a lot of emotions – for example they suffer pain and loss when one of their own dies or is physically hurt. I would say they have moved beyond the fourth dimension and are now ascending into the fifth dimension way of thinking and being, but they have not yet reached the level of the Diacuratians.

They have telepathic powers and spoken language for communication, with the dialects varying slightly around their planet. As time progresses, the spoken languages are becoming less important and their conscious telepathic minds are expanding as they enter the fifth energy frequency. They are a peaceful people, living in communities based on assisting and helping each other, and this has assured their survival. Because of the way this planet is situated within its solar system, enjoying the protection of a larger planet, they benefit from a lovely temperate climate.

Their light days and dark nights are shorter than ours and they do not live by time-restricting their lives – they have ascended beyond that now. There was a time when their civilisation was more focused on time keeping, but they have now grown out of the third dimension limited way of thinking and see everything differently. As you can imagine, the ascension of this planet has been very interesting to the Intergalactic Council and the overseers. After attuning to their history files, I would also say that these beings never had the destructive tendency to hurt each other in the first place.

Their planet has a lighter gravity with thinner air, and they have learnt to adapt and live off the energy sources of their planet. Their form resembles ours with limbs and a similar physical make-up, but if you saw them this light day, you would see a glow around them. I noticed the males and females are similar in appearance, but the females are more delicate in features and slightly smaller. They have silver-grey hair and smooth, pale lilac skin. Just above their brow is a section of skin over their bone structure that protrudes out and then recedes back, which is the start of their hairline. The hair is straight and usually long for both sexes. They have three long fingers and a thumb on each hand, and four toes on the end of long feet.

They have learnt to tap into their planet's energy source to aid their physical energy existence. They nourish themselves and fuel their energy levels with what I would best describe to you as a vegetable diet, along with the energy source connection from their planet. The plant life source creates energy as well as a source for the air they breathe, and it's this combination that helps them survive. They have never eaten the creatures of their world, even in their primitive past, as they have always respected and worshipped the nature of their planet.

Castrolian is a clean planet; they have clean energy and their power source for heat and lighting is produced from their natural resources such as their light star and wind power. Because of how they are developed and their deep-rooted respect for what the planet provides, they have never harmed their life source, taking only what they need for survival, while giving thanks to their planet.

I was interested in how they produce their young, and discovered they carry the seed of life within each gender; when they meet the mate of their choice, they choose the right moment to have their young. The female of their species releases an egg cocooned in a transparent hard shell, which comes from an organ that looks like a small gill on the side of her body; the male then releases pods from his gill that sprinkle over the shell of the egg and fertilise it. The shell is then safely placed in an environment incubator connected to the planet's life source. Tentacles form from the shell to link to the planet source of life force energy and as it does, the outer shell turns a light purple. The young being is nourished by this planet energy source, helping the shell and young Castrolian being to grow, developing its gender, individual essence and character while cocooned in its own shell.

When the Castrolian being is ready to be born, the hard shell changes colour to a dark purple and it cracks open. The young Castrolian being is lifted out and separated from its energy source, which has been connected to the gill on the right hand side of their body. The young being then starts its life with its family group.

From their side gill they have silvery tentacles that connect to certain plant sources that provide the energy source to recharge. The best way to describe this is that they connect to huge tree-like plants that grow around their planet. If you could see these huge plants, you would see a glow of energy that pulsates through them like blood in veins, and this is what the Castrolians link into. The trees produce vines that reach wherever they are needed and this is how the young feed too. When they are around a year old, the young start to consume plant matter for the other nutrients they need.

Telcarian told me they have the equivalent of lungs and heart, and the liquid in their veins has a translucent glow to it. They have a food filtration system in their body for digestion. Castrolians mate for life as we do and have one or two younglings; they are drawn to their partner by an inner connection, quite often bonding when young. I was lucky enough to observe a matching ceremony, which is witnessed by their whole community. At these ceremonies they play music through long crystal pipes and they dance too; believe me, this is beautiful to hear and see. The experience reminded me of my own planet, especially the crystal musical instruments.

Castrolians wear mostly practical garments to cover up their form, made from a plant that they process and weave into fabric. They also like to decorate their non-working clothes with gems and crystals, which are easily found on the planet's surface, especially near the flowing energy sources. On special occasions of celebration, they also use their world's flora to decorate their hair and homes, appreciating the beauty of their nature.

They live in communities, in individual single story dwellings. Their dwelling lighting comes from a crystal that absorbs the light stars energy and reflects the light outwards when it's dark. They also have another crystal stone that gives out heat absorbed from the planet's energies and light star, which is used for a mixture of warmth and cooking. I think what I love about this planet is how it provides, through natural resources that work in harmony with the Castrolians.

Their main source of travel is flight, for which they use a clean, crystal-based energy source with rechargeable properties. Their flight machines do not have wings – they use a power that raises them from the ground and propels them to their destination. They also have boat crafts as they enjoy their equivalent of a water source on their planet, and these crafts hover across the flat energy lakes as well as the flat parts of land. The machines are made from a single mineral source that can be manipulated to their needs. Extraction of this is closely monitored and comes from one part of their planet.

They sleep in their dwellings mainly to rest their minds; during sleep, the tentacles from their gills plug into their planet's source of energy, a vine-like growth that comes from a special plant already described.

The planet is alive and full of energy; deep-set into its crystal cores is the recorded history of the Castrolians and their teachings. Through time, the physical beings of the planet connected to this source for life and education. The knowledge that is held within the planet's crystal cores is transferred to the energy source for the Castrolians to absorb. This is akin to transferring a planet's DNA pattern of thought, and they have also learnt to telepathically transfer knowledge and images into crystals. They use shafts of crystal about eighteen inches long and one inch across; they are hexagonal and placed into their technology, which reflects this information in images around the user, or it can connect to their thought patterns. Due to their ascension level, they can now take themselves into the situation or the subject, and experience it as if they are part of it, similar to a virtual reality experience.

As for illness, Castrolians have different types of bacteria on their planet that can cause them to feel off-colour, but they use thought and natural remedies to heal themselves. It is mostly old age that takes them from their families; their bodies wear out but they do live longer than they used to and we see this increasing in their future timeline.

On Castrolian, there are Councils that oversee each of the planet's six main city areas. There are also smaller population pockets scattered around the planet, for example in areas of specific activity such as food growth or crystal mining. The Councils are made up of twelve elders, elected for their experience to ensure community values are maintained, and that they are taught to the young. Remember the access to the universe knowledge library; this has shown them new technologies and other planets, but with their clarity of thinking, they know to take only what serves them for the best – their method of flight, for example, was an idea that came from this library. They also know not to invite less ascended beings to visit their planet, or take on new technologies that they don't understand, or that will not serve the greater good, as this would destabilise their way of life. So they protect themselves, and they are now ascended to this early fifth dimension energy level, bringing unity and love, with no greed or harm to others.

I must not forget their nature and animal kingdom, as it is beautiful. The most similar animals to ours are the winged mammals, but they are taller with longer necks, running in herds, and highly spiritual creatures. There are creatures very like cats, as well as flying creatures that live off the nectar of plants, and creatures that burrow into the ground. There are predators, too, which live off each other as well as off vegetation and the planet energy source. There is a natural order to things in their animal kingdom, which if uninterrupted helps keep the animal populations under control. Their habitats remain untouched and the planet's nature is allowed to stay balanced, as the Castrolians understand that for their survival, it is important the planet is unpolluted. The animals live in harmony with the Castrolians, and connected to the planet source of energy; through their evolution, all of these beautiful beings understand this connection.

In the universal knowledge library recordings, Telcarian showed me the amazing moment in Castrolian's history when the Salcaritons stepped forward to reveal their connection with them. Through their ascension, the Castrolians have telepathically connected to the Salcaritons and to the universal knowledge library, and have decided as a collective that there are certain things they do not want to introduce into their world to protect it. This is because it would threaten their peaceful existence; with their great foresight and knowledge, this makes Castrolian quite an amazing place to visit.

I hope you enjoyed my simple explanation of this beautiful planet; I hope to go back to Castrolian one day and actually meet these beautiful beings myself – and become friends with them.

Life Journal – transmission 18 - 'The light within Atlantis'

I just had to come on my journal and tell you about the last couple of light days of multidimensional travel. I was very honoured because Ioliismiem took me to his home planet, Arcturus. This Arcturian home planet is a blue jewel and reminds me of Earth in some ways. Arcturus is larger and orbits a red giant star in an area known as Bootes Constellation.

Arcturus is a fifth dimensional planet; this means that the planet itself, its creatures and the Arcturians have shed the third and fourth dimensional energy to live in the fifth energy dimension. They are at various stages of evolution and ascension; some stay in physical bodies, some are in between physical lives, vibrating in the ninth dimension, and choosing when to move back into physical form on their planet and in the universe. Ioliismiem has chosen to visit our planet in physical form, so we can relate to him better. Those that adopt physical form can stay in their bodies much longer than we do, usually existing in these forms for between 200 and 300 Earth years. Ioliismiem compared their evolution to ours, as they were contacted by the overseers over a million hyons ago, and took their first steps towards the divine light source as we did. I was reminded that our planet is also at different stages of ascension evolutions, and it is the natural order for some species to progress this way.

The Arcturians travel in two types of star ships. The first is made of pure light and harmonic sound which they connect with their energy frequency, and becomes part of their energy. The second is for Arcturians in physical form; they travel in solid ships using light way portals to travel long distances.

I arrived on the planet at night and the living and working structures looked intriguing to me in the dark, shiny against the stars as the clear night sky reflected on them. The buildings were impressive, strong, angular and some were pyramid-shaped. In the daylight, they were even more beautiful, constructed from a white crystalline material, which glowed and sparkled in the light of their light star. The surface reflects everything like a mirror, so the buildings seem to change all the time. I discovered the energy they use is derived from light and crystals, which powers all their needs.

Ioliismiem told me that when an Arcturian reaches maturity, they are allocated their role in society according to their energy colour vibrations. They also have families, and their younglings or children for your understanding are now created in the eighth dimension. Specific Arcturians with a violet energy vibration are given the role of creating children, and being their teachers. This guardian role is highly esteemed. With each new generation the young expand their conscious energy even further, and I would say that this is the most important function on their planet. When the children are ready they go to their allocated families for nurturing and upbringing. Their families also come together for the purpose of creating a shared experience and learning from each other.

To me, their civilization seems to function seamlessly. Each Arcturian knows their role and purpose, fulfilling the needs of all without materialistic needs. They are also a self-healing race, using light and energy to heal themselves, working with the vibration of colour and the energy of sound to help them.

During the quick tour of this planet, I noticed the high amount of water that covered it and the lush areas of trees, plants and beautiful flowers. Their animal kingdom is very diverse as well, with many varieties of species. I discovered that all beings of various intelligence levels on Arcturus live in harmony, no one species owning another, and they are all sentient beings that love and protect each other.

Their oceans are also filled with species of various intelligence levels. I was told that dolphins and whales originate from Arcturus, and were introduced into Atlantis in the second experiment to help raise the energies of the planet Earth.

When I asked Ioliismiem about his own family unit, he told me he had not yet taken a partner to create a family unit, as he continually travels the universe helping the overseers and Intergalactic Council with their work. But he said that when the time is right he will fulfil this part of his destiny. I realised he does not live within any time constraints, his purpose is for the now and the unconditional love he can give to all he comes in contact with. He is a warrior, not in the fighting sense, but in the sense of his convictions and passion for what he believes in. He is a protector of many species, especially in the experiments concerning humanity and what they could become.

Life Journal – transmission 19 - 'The light within Atlantis'

I cannot believe how the light days are flying by; I feel I have been neglecting everything apart from Dolso. My parents have been around the Temple and we have had some telepathic linked catch-ups, but not the physical contact I now seem to need. So we set aside this light day for this purpose. Zogica has also been trying to reach me through the crystals, and when I spoke with him, he had very exciting news.

He showed me his finished drawings for the Creatorion he has designed for creational purposes of the arts. He creates flat plans as well as three-five Dimensional visual views that you can project and walk through in your mind. It will be a very beautiful complex of buildings and outside spaces – a mixture of clear crystal structures for performances and white sparkling crystal stone carved with the art that reflects our world. The gardens will have flowing energy water pools and cascades into ponds, outside seating areas, and the amphitheatre he hopes to include. They have submitted the plans to the Sacred Light Council for approval and he is waiting to hear the outcome, which should be in a few light days.

He told me he had been on a light star ship to Arcturian to look at the architecture for inspiration and building techniques. He spent a couple of light days there and sounded in awe of these beautiful people and their planet. I had never seen him so enthusiastic, as if a new light had gone on inside him. Zogica also explained they were going to show us how to construct the buildings, manifesting the materials, and carving them with laser power from light and harmonic sound. I must say I am very proud of his achievements and look forward to the light day I can walk in this beautiful space he has designed.

After our meal, I showed my parents the designs and three-five dimensional viewing tour of Creatorion; they were also very impressed and proud of his achievement so far, and thought the designs were outstanding. We were also thrilled at the proposed name of the site: Alcerian Touliza Creatorion. He wanted to reflect our beautiful nature, the path of light and me in the name, and I was very honoured.

It was lovely to catch up with my parents and update them on my experiences of multidimensional travel. They are fully informed of what's occurring, but it's good to get different perspectives on these events. I could see my father was in his element as he told me he had been busy greeting off-world species coming to view the Atlantis mission, and my mother had been occupied with the Temple teachings. This had increased due to more of my people advancing their multidimensional techniques, thanks to the interest in the Atlantis mission and the possible future incarnation programme.

Dolso also enjoyed the day of extra attention. He was actually making many friends, and being entertained when I could not be with him. There were many other creatures at the Temple; he had befriended one in particular, a feline cat creature called Harsen, a gentle sleek giant who is rusty red in colour and follows Dolso around in the gardens, playing with him. It is wonderful to see him so happy and well.

Life Journal – transmission 20 - 'The light within Atlantis'

My energy is spinning with excitement at these multidimensional travels. Most of the third dimensional planets we are visiting are from scientific observational viewpoints only, and the planets are unaware we are there as we explore them. The high dimensional planets and realms are aware of our visit and welcome us to study their home worlds. We only visit civilisations that are under the care of the Intergalactic Council, as they are safe destinations. Unfortunately, there are aggressive, selfish species, also highly ascended, that we are protected from by the Arcturians, who protect these planets and realms on behalf of the Intergalactic Council, as their star ships are superior to all that are known to us at the moment.

The next planet I want to tell you about is called Xerioc One. This planet fascinates the master scientists and astrologists, as it defies the general makeup of planets that support life.

Xerioc One orbits a light star, but there are two light stars in the same solar system opposite each other. They both have planets rotating around them but amazingly, the opposing gravitational pull of these systems does not cause the stars and planets to collide. Xerioc One orbits the smaller of the two light stars. The outside of the planet is made up of floating asteroids and ice rocks of various sizes, which are continuously moving. Within this is a small planet with an atmosphere, while the exosphere sits below the layer of floating asteroid rocks. Through this planet is a core of rock made up of various elements that merge from the planet on the north and south poles. This extends up into the exosphere, connecting with the asteroid rocks belt of energy. It's an amazing sight to see all this rotating around the light star.

This is a green planet with water and landmass. The species here are giant beings in the early stages of physical third dimensional energy, at a level of basic agricultural development. They have large heads, large trunk bodies, long arms and short legs, and male and female gender. Their skin looks grey and warty, and their hair is a rusty red. They have green eyes and communicate through a verbal language; they have no technology or written word. They seek leadership of their communities through fighting which could involve either gender, and at the moment, the stronger of the two wins. I also observed caring family environments for the young. The males and females were the workers of the land and the females were also more of the homemakers. Both genders are very strong and hard working.

It is a very fertile planet, yielding an abundance of food. From what I observed they live in village communities with varying levels of feuds and peace amongst them.

Their landscape is amazing; they have very high-rising, spiked mountains that drop away to large valleys with freshwater lakes and flat landmasses. There are no oceans, but huge waterfalls that drop away to large lake areas, and the beings all live near these water sources. They also have huge trees in massive forest areas. Their animal kingdom varies, but is mainly dominated by large land mammals that they hunt for fur and meat. These people see their animals as a food source, not pets, but they know to take only what they need for survival. This shows us they are in the early stages of developing respect for their planet. I think it is one of the most dramatic landscapes I have seen so far, but breathtakingly beautiful.

Planet Xerioc One is a recent find by the intergalactic explorers and has not yet been selected for incarnation. They are only observed at the moment for the scientific information they can provide regarding the makeup of their planet and the unusual light stars. I have discovered that the observation of planets, with no contact to alter their direction, is very common. I am not sure at the moment of all the criteria they need to qualify for incarnation or a visit from the overseers. But one thing I do know – if they are showing basic respect for their planet, that is definitely one of the requirements.

Life Journal – transmission 21 -
'The light within Atlantis'

One of the things I have been doing on my breaks from my training has been exploring the Sacred Light Temple. This light day I went to the area my mother works in for the advancement of meditation leading to multidimensional travel. As our people ascend and show signs of advanced telepathic mind state, they are invited to the Temple for training to advance their ascension. This decision is based on free will, so it is their choice alone if they feel it's time to take that path. If they choose not to when invited, they are given guidance to help them to move towards this next level of advancement. Remember the doubt energy; this can hold us back and create the fear of not being ready for that next leap, and it still holds our planet back from full ascension.

The area of the Temple my mother works in is very beautiful, and my favourite part is the healing and meditation area. The rooms are tranquil spaces with vibrations of sound and light. These can be set at the frequencies needed for each individual to achieve deep relaxation and take their mind into the clarity of the now moment that is needed for further development. The walls are painted with nature scenes from our planet, in the natural and vibrant tones we see around us. We have some very talented artists among us that express the beauty of our planet in a very creative way. They use ore paints mixed from ground minerals and crystals. When mixed, some of these create the most vibrant shimmering colours you can imagine that reflect our floribunda. These rooms open out onto terraces with lush plant life and running water, creating another beautiful space to find your true connection.

Off these rooms are others, rather like the one I described that we are using for the multidimensional travel training. They are set up in a similar way but without the viewing platform. There is something wonderful about the energy in this space my mother works in, and I feel the best word I can use to describe it is serenity.

I am very delighted at the moment, as my mother told me today that Zogica's mind and multidimensional travel training have exceeded her expectations. She knows it's because of his bond link experience with me at the Alcerian Touliza Mountains, and his energy pathways have opened up to allow this new experience. He has been invited to join my mother at the Temple on regular light day sessions to enhance his development. This means I will see more of him, which is wonderful news. I have spoken to him and the Creatorion plans were approved, so he is overseeing those. When they are further along, he will have time for more training with my mother for multidimensional travel and separation.

Life Journal – transmission 22 -
'The light within Atlantis'

The next planet I was taken to we call Zelcriton, which means the floating planet. The centre of this unusual planet is made up of gases, liquid and solid form surrounded by a gravity field. Within this dense gravity field, islands float all around the planet at different heights in the atmosphere; although they vary in size, they move at the same pace and are held on fixed courses. Some of the islands have tiers, connected by rock formations with plant life, and an energy source that flows between them which looks like a pulsating, glowing fluorescent river of liquid.

I asked Telcarian how this unusual planet came about. He told me that many millennia ago it was hit by an interstellar rogue planet that came into its solar system. Rogue planets are objects that have been ejected from their home planetary system, or have never been gravitationally bound to any light star. The universe is full of them, and it's rare to find an advanced life form on them without a light star for protection.

When the rogue planet hit, Zelcriton reacted by breaking up. It shifted orbit around its light star, creating a heavier gravity which held the planet in its own magnetic field. The rogue planet carried on through its solar system, not causing any more destruction.

When the planet was hit it had lower level animal and insect life forms living on its surface. The ones that survived this impact slowly evolved over thousands of years and adapted to living on the floating islands. Because of the gases, the centre of the planet was uninhabitable at first, but it did eventually settle, with some primitive life thriving in the new conditions.

From these creatures evolved a species of intelligent flying beings. They are no more than three feet in height, with beautiful opaque wings that fold away down their backs. Their heads and eyes remind me of the lizard found on some planets including Earth. They have ear and airway holes and mouth, legs, arms and a slim tail, with a scaly skin of blue and green tones. They walk, climb and fly and have adapted well to their environment. They also build their resting places on the underside of the floating islands, which are like organised hives, and they have adapted to live in family groups. After observation I found out they ate plant life, small flying insects and mammals. They catch them with fine, very strong woven web nets, made from a material that comes from vines, which can be pulled apart into many fine strings. It's like air fishing, I decided – a lot of the second dimensional life is air bound, as that is how they have learned to survive and evolve to move about the planet. There are also ground creatures, and some nocturnal animals.

The species of intelligent flying beings is telepathic in nature, conducting communication through thought. We found this quite fascinating, as this ability is usually found in the progression of a species, which has ascended to the fourth and fifth dimensions. They have also evolved into communities with a leader, protectors and workers. Remember the second dimension of animal and plant life; well, they have ascended into the third primitive dimension. I say primitive as they have no technology, and have not yet realised the power of, say, crystals and their light star. But the way they are advancing, we predict it will not be long before one of them has a light moment of clarity and they take that next leap in their ascension.

Telcarian and Ioliismiem both say the Intergalactic Council is closely watching their development because of the telepathic communication, and from the scientific perspective, how this broken up planet reformed into what it is now. I can understand this, as it is a fascinating place to observe.

Life Journal – transmission 23 -
'The light within Atlantis'

The last forty days have flown by, I feel as if my feet haven't touched the ground. I suppose they haven't, really, as I've spent a lot of time multidimensional travelling! I am meeting with the mission team tomorrow to review the multidimensional progress. Today, I am transmitting my report on how I think it went, for them to review before the meeting.

The report I have transmitted is extensive, and will be attached to the journal transmission files in the future, but for now I will tell you my immediate thoughts. I suppose my starting point is the success of this last forty days, which started with conquering my self-doubt lower energy; once that had been pushed aside my energies soared, enabling me to put my full trust in Telcarian, Ioliismiem and the mission team.

I now fully understand the power of my mind, including the power of the intent of thought, which helped me choose destinations for multidimensional travelling. I also understand the power of the full multidimensional energy link connecting the mind to the physical body, enabling you to maintain the link throughout separation. The intent is set at the highest energy matrix of the twelfth dimension, and links back through all dimensions, stopping at the reference point of existence you are in. Imagine silver threads from the divine source, which your multidimensional body is tethered to, weaving their way through the cosmic universe to your physical body. This powerful thought cannot be broken unless the mind setting the event chooses it; the physical body dies during multidimensional travelling, or another being of high ascension energy links to your frequency to intervene if you are in danger.

With these multidimensional experiences my consciousness has grown, and my individual ascension level has now increased. Telcarian said I was approaching my mother's level of ascension very quickly; they had been impressed by how my energy has purified to let in the unconditional love energy of the divine source from the sixth to twelfth dimensions. They conclude from this that with each new generation the powers are getting stronger, with quicker results once the energies are aligned and cleared of any doubt and other negative influences.

I do feel different; although I am still at my fifth dimension physical existence level, and choose to stay here, but I could now shed my physical body and stay in my ethereal light multidimensional existence if I wished. Ioliismiem estimates that in around three to four generations we will be like the Arcturians – whose existence I discussed in an earlier transmission.

Today, we gathered in the multidimensional training chambers with the mission team and some observers from the Intergalactic Council. Our journey of the last forty light days was viewed and our transmission reports were discussed at great length. I could feel an underlying excitement, but also the seriousness of this mission to Atlantis.

The purpose of today was for the mission team, ascended science masters, and Intergalactic Council members to decide if I was ready for the next phase of the experiment. This was to take my multidimensional self and create a mini self-version for incarnation in the chosen humanoid form on Atlantis. I hope the translation does the explanation of this next amazing event justice, for all individuals who are downloading the transmissions in whatever form and language.

The answer back from the meeting was yes, I was ready to take the next step. Telcarian, Ioliismiem, Catelifon and Avielil explained to me what would happen next, which would involve me linking with a humanoid form conceived in Atlantis; they also explained that not all human babies survive birth, or can pass away just after, in very rare cases.

The healing is wonderful in Atlantis so the reasons for these rare cases vary – one being that the incarnating energies do not blend well and cause the mother's physical body to reject the human foetus. Another more recent reason is genetic breakdown, where the foetus cannot develop properly. In the first experiment this was not an issue, as the children were created off-world, and given to the non-gender family groups. Once they introduced two genders and creating generation after generation, defects through DNA breakdown happened on rare occasions that could cause the child to die in the womb or just after birth. It was suggested that this was because the Atlantis experiment was falling into the lower energies, causing more disease and degeneration of the humanoid form, which was not connected to the high source healing energy.

We know now that as a race, we have what is called a higher self; this is my multidimensional link with the creation of source. This pure unconditional love energy that we have been able to recognise and connect with, now guides us in our ascension. It has brought us away from materialistic values, persuasion and hold over others and a judgemental way of thinking, changing our behaviour patterns to bring harmony to our people. When I create my other self to be incarnated, I will be the higher self to which it will connect.

Avielil's people have the developed technique for this separation to happen, using a mixture of light and harmonic sound energy and my power of thought to create the twin me. He explained the three selves present in the Atlantis humanoid form. The actual self is their everyday functioning mind – pretty much everything they think and do. The body self is the physical realisation of the 'I am', although it works in conjunction with the actual self. The higher self is the observer and evaluator of the other two selves, the incarnated energy linking with me. When all three are working in balance, a species copes and moves in harmony of life. To create this harmony it is vital the incarnation transition is balanced.

When I say creating a twin, it is not an identical copy of my multidimensional body, but more of a reflection of myself, that is linked to me at all times. My reflection of self will be a multidimensional vessel that will be the gatherer of knowledge and information from my incarnated life on the physical Earth plane. We will be linked at all times, but I will choose when to connect and see the progression of my physical Earth life. When my reflection of self returns at the end of my Earth life, everything is reviewed and downloaded into our transmission library and up to the intergalactic knowledge library. I will then reconnect with my reflection of self.

I plan to continue transmitting my Atlantean life to my journal in the current format, choosing the key moments to share with you while living my Diacuratian existence. The full life transmission will be available separately to connect to, relaying every moment and feeling of that Earth lifetime for those who wish to study it.

Life Journal – transmission 24 –
'The light within Atlantis'

I have just come back from a walk with my father and Dolso to be informed by Telcarian that they will carry out the multidimensional separation in four light days' time. While I wait, I will be spending some of that time with my mother in her Temple meditation multidimensional chambers, meditating and working on my energies so they are fully balanced. I am also secretly excited, as Zogica is going to take some time away from the Creatorian project to be with me. Hopefully nobody will mind, as long as I do my work with my mother.

It was lovely to spend time with my father today and see him so happy in his work. As one of our ambassadors, he has been kept busy with off-world visitors, welcoming them to the Sacred Light Temple and making sure their needs are catered for. We have had more visitors because of the Atlantean experiment – many of them are observers of this special event and us. Interestingly, my father said that some were from planets similar to ours, and on our ascension level, and were considering if they wished to become involved in the incarnation programme of the Intergalactic Council.

I had not realised the Atlantean incarnation was something our elders on Diacurat had been considering for a while. While making this decision, they had also travelled as observers to other planets, which had chosen to take the first steps to incarnate on Earth and other planets. If my incarnation is successful, the experience will also be offered out to others of my species. Our people will never make a decision that does not benefit the whole, only bringing knowledge that will aid our ascension into the unconditional love energy.

Life Journal – transmission 25 -
'The light within Atlantis'

It was so lovely to see Zogica this light day; he bought me a beautiful gift – a necklace of Silienia crystals. They are the most beautiful crystals; they reflect the world around them, including colours, your energy and vibration. If you concentrate on the crystals, you see their energy moving within them, which is quite hypnotic. These are rare on our planet and I feel honoured to receive them as a gift from someone who loves me. It's the first gift Zogica has made to me; he said it was to seal our bonding, and they will remind me of him when we are not together. I did not have the heart to tell him I did not need an object to be reminded of him and his love. But the sweet gesture of grace pulsated his love out to me and that is wonderful.

We spent the light day by ourselves just being, enjoying each other's company and making plans for our future. The main topic was our bonding ceremony, which will be held after my Atlantis mission has come to an end. A bonding ceremony takes place at an allotted moment and this light day we asked permission for the ceremony to be held at the Temple when the time comes. Bonding ceremonies are beautiful events reflecting the true love of the two beings joining in this long life bond of love and beyond.

We also reflected on the love energy today and what it means to us both. We concluded the love is energy of purity, binding us all together across the universe. Your love for each other can be so strong it can overwhelm individuals at times, and the experience of it can be measured in your state of wellbeing. Love is not just from the pheromonic and cellular structure of the physical body; it is always part of you. This love lets you glow from within and also radiates on your outer being. When you find this love it radiates out and changes your persona so that others see you differently, and your perception of others is different, too.

It was so wonderful to have this time with Zogica today, as I saw a deeper, more connected side of him I had not seen before. He is fun-loving, calm and hard-working, but he has a very spiritual, deep side to him that's starting to emerge. I feel the work he has started doing with my mother has helped his connection and brought him understanding of what we do here in the Sacred Light Temple for the good of our citizens and our planet.

Life Journal – transmission 26 –
'The light within Atlantis'

I thought I had better take some moments to update my journal about my multidimensional split that took place a few light days ago, and was quite an experience. I arrived at the special chamber that had been created for this under the supervision of Telcarian, Ioliismiem, Catelifon and Avielil. A lot of what we have achieved so far with the Atlantis mission had been open to observation, but on the advice of Avielil, based on his experience, it was decided that this part should be done in a controlled environment with only the people with a direct involvement attending. The event would then be shared afterwards to the appropriate beings.

First of all, I had to lie down in a monitoring pod that would observe my physical body functions. When everything was ready to go, I was asked to separate into my multidimensional self. I then had to place my multidimensional self in the light harmonic sound particle transmitter. This is an open, round column space, and when I enter it, I am surrounded by a light harmonic sound beam. My multidimensional self is monitored at the same time as my physical self. They observe the energy link between physical and ethereal form by monitoring my energy frequency vibration, which is unique for every being in the universe, and make sure it stays stable.

While the light harmonic sound beam surrounded me, I could feel my ethereal self pulsating. My mind was focused on the thought intent of the split, which would create a reflection of me. Then I heard a sound that was new to me and the light beams started to throb and spin around me. I felt as if someone was pulling at my energy and I heard Avielil's voice telling me to release, I was meant to have no expectations, trust and go with the feelings that came across me. I felt myself change, felt a bit weaker than normal and it was taking everything I had to stay focused. Then I felt the light harmonic sound beams slow and clear and Avielil asked me to return to my physical body.

I was left to sleep, which was welcome, as I was a little drained from the experience. When I woke up the room was a hive of activity. In the middle of the room, there was a light being that was an energy reflection of me. The form was different to my multidimensional self; it was like a floating pulsation ball of light. I could feel it was part of me and in my mind I could see what my self-reflection was feeling and seeing. Avielil said I would telepathically connect to my reflection of self as I do to any physical being, but as well as hearing communication in my mind I would see images of where they were. I can also control when this happens as I lead my life here in the Temple.

The next stage was to place my energy connection reflection of self into the chosen humanoid foetus on Earth and test that everything is functioning as it should be.

Avielil explained to me they had found that for the humanoid form, the best way of blending with the foetus was gradually, over a few Earth weeks. By week twenty-four of a human pregnancy, the foetus is usually fully formed, and at this point, the reflection of self will be completed and functioning fully within. During the weeks that the incarnated energy is gaining strength, I will be connecting, observing what my refection self can feel and see. I cannot express to you in words how much I am looking forward to this unique experience.

Life Journal – transmission 27 -
'The light within Atlantis'

Following the split of my multidimensional self it was normal to monitor the physical body, multidimensional self and reflection of self for a while to make sure all was stable. This took a couple of our light days. My life form in Atlantis had been selected and all was ready to proceed to the next stage.

I was to be incarnated into a foetus, known on Earth as a baby, who will be named Aigle – which means light and radiance – and the Earth year of my birth will be 9950 BC. She is part of a high-ranking Atlantean family, and would be the youngest child of Antonioni and Gisela. I will reveal to you more about her life as it unfolds.

It was now time for me to blend my reflection of self with the Earth baby. We used a light way portal to reach Earth in Avielil's light star ship, and from there, my reflection of self will blend with the Earth baby. Avielil's light star ship is at the fifth physical dimensional level, created for helping fifth dimensional species in these procedures. It has similar chambers to those that were set up on Diacurat in the Temple. I was part of this procedure as my thoughts would help guide my reflection of self to the host being, with the use of Avielil's light harmonic sound technology.

Avielil explained to us that they would not place all of my reflection of self into the baby at one go, as the physical shock within the womb could cause a bad reaction. As Aigle grows in the womb, more of my refection of self will be slowly filtered into her. The master scientists have found that the soul within split between human and spirit becomes balanced within the human form, although the time this event takes place, can be different for each human.

Throughout my mission with this physical form, I will be supported by guidance and healing from Telcarian, Ioliismiem, Avielil and my mother. This is to ensure my own physical body stays in balance with my mind and maintains the stable link to my reflection of self. The chamber was silent as this was carried out; only beings that were to help with connecting to the event taking place were present, and my first journey in an incarnated form began.

My reflection of self was in the light harmonic sound technology transporter, with myself, Telcarian, Ioliismiem and Avielil surrounding it; physically and in mind, we were linked as one. These three friends were my guiding strength and would remain with me throughout this Earth life as guides. I felt my own energy alter but remained connected to my reflection of self and my guiding group. My thoughts were as one with them, and we shared the experience with my reflection of self as it went to the chosen Earth being in her mother's womb.

I was aware of everything the baby was feeling, from her cellular structure, physical sensations, her blood pumping through her veins, and her developing mind feelings, which extended to awareness of the world outside the womb. All of this information was being fed back to me, as my reflection of self is like a recording sponge, soaking up all that happens. When my reflection of self was stable we all drew back our energy and Avielil could then monitor the completion of the connection using the light harmonic sound technology transporter. My reflections of self's transmissions of energy were now going to be collected by the mission group, who could also watch Aigle's life as it progressed. But what was of real interest to the master scientists was to see how I would feel and respond to my incarnated refection of self – known by the humans on Earth as a soul.

My first observation was how tranquil the being Aigle felt – she had no past or future thoughts or expectations, she was living in the now moment of reality. She only could feel the unconditional love of source and her mother. She also felt vibrations from the outside world coming through the womb, but as of yet they had no meaning to her. I realised baby humanoids have no perceived ideas; she would enter the Earth world dependent on her parents for survival. I can relate this to our own world, as it is similar for many physical existing species across the universe.

I now had to wait patiently for when the newborn baby chose to leave the womb and start her new life on her Earth path. I felt fine, even though a part of my energy was leaving for a period of time to be in the physical form, and I felt comforted by knowing we would always be connected.

Avielil also mentioned that when the child is born, her soul – my reflection of self – could leave the physical body while she slept and explore the Earth. So the soul is not cocooned for the Earth years in the moments we spend within the physical body. The term given to this is astral travelling, and all the incarnated souls can have outer body experiences while the human form is sleeping or in a deep meditative state. I also can spend time in the fourth dimension astral plane and connect with my fifth dimension energy friends. My reflection of self is tethered to her Earth body as my ethereal energy is to mine.

When we arrived back at Diacurat there was a welcoming

committee, and everyone was delighted at the success so far of this incarnation. My parents were especially pleased to see me and had arranged a gathering of celebration for all those involved in this Atlantean mission. After some delightful creative entertainment, delicious food and all the conversations, I did feel tired and managed to slip away to see Dolso. We cuddled in my rest chamber and I drifted off into a deep sleep.

Life Journal – transmission 28 –
'The light within Atlantis'

Now my reflection of self was safely installed in Aigle and my energies were balanced, I was free to be part of the light Temple community, and within reason, moving about as I wanted. My connection to Aigle is always with me and whenever I wish I can tap into the soul frequency and see what's been happening in her human life. Aigle's parents are her physical Earth guardians, and between me and my reflection of self, we will guide the human form through her life with the assistance of Telcarian, Ioliismiem, Avielil, Catelifon and the twelve Celestial Guardian beings of Atlantis.

If my reflection's self-consciousness needs guidance, Telcarian, Ioliismiem, Avielil, Catelifon and my multidimensional self will be called upon to assist. I will sense my reflection of self-energy and any frequencies that waver within her. I have to be on hand quickly if needed, which is why they want me in the Temple vicinity during the first mission.

I will spend time every light day connecting fully with my reflection of self and downloading the transmission from her to view. I will report any significant moments in her life, along with my experiences. When this mission is finished the complete lifeline of Aigle will be available from the knowledge library of Intergalactic Council on request.

On top of all this excitement, I have had the delight of seeing Zogica this light day. He showed me captured images of the Alcerian Touliza Creatorion. The crystalline structures are well on the way to completion and they were starting the ground works for the outside recreational and creative performing areas. He explained all the technical difficulties that he had been required to solve. I have to admit this did not excite me much, but I kept listening, as it was wonderful to see the excitement in his eyes as he resolved the problems all on his own.

He also told me about a new colleague, Axhan, from the planet called Drygonmi. Axhan was skilled at designing and building structures and star ships on his home planet, and had come to observe Zogica's design and construction methods for the Creatorion, and we felt this was a high compliment indeed for him.

Zogica described the Drygonmi race as a lot smaller than us with humanoid form – four limbs and a larger head, with a skin that had a scaly texture similar to certain fish species. They come from a highly advanced, peaceful world, travelling the universe as explorers in light star ships. They come from a system with a luminous blue star and their planet exists in a spiral galaxy, similar to Earth's.

They communicate with us telepathically and they have passed on their knowledge to many species across the universe Delta. Their influences can also be seen on Earth in the intergalactic library, where species have colonised Earth in the past before the Atlantis experiments. They have also been interacting with the Celestial Guardians of Atlantis and have been the foundation of influence in the building advancement of Atlantis on Earth. They are also aware of the incarnation programme and are thinking of becoming part of it.

After Zogica described this species, I actually realised I had seen a couple of them on the observation platform in the multidimensional chamber, but not yet linked with them. I must say hello if I see them again.

Life Journal – transmission 29 –
'The light within Atlantis'

This is a momentous light day, when Aigle, my chosen human form, is born on Earth. There was so much excitement at the Temple today as we all observed this event on the Earth plane. I had wondered at this little human's path in Atlantis and I was told she had been given a DNA strain that gave her a higher purpose, which had also been given to other humans who had become priests or priestesses. They had been working on this DNA strain in the hope it would prove to be more powerful, helping the human being bring the unconditional love and light needed to save the experiment. This helped set her destiny on her life's path, hopefully with the desired outcome required by the ascension scientists and Intergalactic Council.

The labour, as Earthlings call this event, started with Gisela's – the mother's – waters breaking. This is a fluid substance that keeps the humanoid sustained with a cord of life from the mother's womb. I witnessed a few Earth hours of the mother in great pain, but this was eased by the healing and herbs she was given while they all waited for this transition of life.

My reflective self was aware of change and the baby's physical body was being squeezed down the human birth canal. This was my first sensation of human pain which I experienced as her head emerged into the world. Then her physical body was out and I felt her take her first breath and express herself to the world around her. She definitely had a good pair of lungs on her. As she took her first breath I witnessed the transition of life in the womb to breathing the air around her. It was as if the physical body took a pause, accepted transition, and then carried on in this new environment.

After the birth, Aigle was washed and swathed in a soft silk material and then she was placed in a very ornate, handed down family rocking crib and her father Antonioni came to see her. He was a man in his forty-fourth year, tall and handsome with olive skin and golden hair. He was dressed in a blue robe decorated with ornate gems. He gently ran his finger down Aigle's cheek and said her name out loud. He embraced her mother, who was in her thirty- ninth year with long, blond hair and paler skin; for a humanoid, she had great beauty and presence.

Aigle, the tenth child, had been born into a high status Atlantean family that lived in the shadow of the main Light Temple of Atlantis. Her father was of master high priest status and served on the Light Council. Their family had a long lineage within this role in Atlantis and with each new generation, some were selected to carry on this ascended priest or priestess role. I had realised I was to be part of a very interesting family, and Aigle, judging from early adult conversation around her, was hoped to show the ascended qualities to fulfill her role at the Sacred Light Temple.

Life Journal – transmission 30 –
'The light within Atlantis'

I feel I am now taking this incarnated mission at a lovely energy pace, striking an even balance between Temple life and the Atlantis mission. After the excitement of Aigle's birth, it has settled down to light days' viewings of my reflection of self, and enjoying my link with this Earth being. The scientist part of me is fascinated with how the human form quickly learns and adapts to the world around them.

It does feel surreal at times, when I am viewing my incarnated life; although I get absorbed into the images and feelings I am experiencing, I am also aware of how fascinating it is at the same time. It has been interesting to observe the infant's response to people's voices, and witnessing the first smile. I've also noticed how quickly they learn to cry for food, or for help when they are not happy or comfortable. They, of course, are dependent on the adults of their world for survival, as are the young on our own planet, and the thousands of other physical life forms which exist in this way.

At the moment, Aigle is often placed in a children's nursery, which is part of her parent's home and linked with the Light Temple. There is a lovely lady called Armineni; she is what they call a wet nurse, helping to feed Aigle from the breast, which produces life-giving milk. She has a young baby too, so this helps out Aigle's mother, as she has many Temple roles to fulfill and not much time to devote to Aigle. Armineni has a lovely motherly energy and I noticed Aigle is very calm when she is with her.

Once the children are in the nursery, it is the role of the high priests to start to observe them. They assess each child for their level of spiritual gifts, guiding them to achieve their full potential with their spiritual strengths. From what I have seen of the other children, this brings them self-worth, happiness and connection to where they belong in the Atlantis society. They achieve this through play, creativity and language connection bringing forth their confidence and gifts.

But I have noticed that something is causing an imbalance of energy around Aigle, and I have noticed, too, that sometimes there are low, whispered, worried adult voices around her. I feel that the energy of the beings talking when this happens is not good for the status quo of Atlantis. When I reported this to Telcarian, he said that for quite a while – a few centuries of Earth time – Atlantis had been showing signs of lower ego energies again, just as in the last four experiments. He also said it was steadily getting worse, with some Atlanteans breaking away from their balanced society and forming their own communities away from the cities. These were pockets of self-materialistic groups that had formed and were influencing more and more Atlanteans to that way of thinking. He said the energy I was picking up on was this lower energy, and it was causing worry amongst the Atlanteans still in the high love source energy.

I had not realised this from my factual studies, and it had not yet been revealed in the knowledge library, but the overseers and Intergalactic Council were already well aware of the start of the breakdown of the fifth Atlantis experiment.

Life Journal – transmission 31 -
'The light within Atlantis'

I have been catching up on the world around me today, talking to friends and Zogica. Everyone is doing very well on their individual paths, which is lovely to see. I have seen Zogica often as he now has more time for the multidimensional training. He was very excited, as he's now been through a couple of light way portals with my mother guiding him. He was also delighted when Ioliismiem took him to Arcturian to meet some of the master architects of his civilisation. He was telling me about the crystalline structure of their buildings and how they can manipulate the materials to create whatever they desire. The basic makeup of this crystalline matter is not found on our planet, but he has spoken to our master scientists and they are going to work with the Arcturians to see if we could create something similar from the crystal formulas of our world. We can manipulate our own crystal crafts and materials with thought frequencies to a certain point, but the Arcturians are way ahead in their technology and thought processes. It will be interesting to see how this collaboration of two worlds will influence our society and buildings in the future.

I was also in awe at how the Creatorion project had turned out. It was the most amazing combination of beautiful structures and landscape recreational areas to create a viewing hub for the arts of our planet. It was also for other off-world species to come and showcase their creativity for us all to enjoy. Diacurat was becoming an intergalactic planet welcoming many off-world visitors now, and the Atlantis mission had opened up our existence to many others. This is a very elevating time for Diacurat and I look forward to seeing where this takes our civilisation.

I am also very elevated, as there has been discussion of me leaving the Temple to visit the Creatorion project so I can experience Zogica's achievements first hand. My incarnated link is working really well and my energies are evenly balanced, so Avielil is suggesting they create a moment to go when the area is quiet, so I do not draw attention to myself. He feels if others I know who are not involved in the mission see me there, there will be so many questions asked, it could unbalance me, so I wait for the permission for this to happen.

My observations of Aigle have been very interesting and I am getting to know her family and their position in the Atlantis society. As I have already said her family has a long lineage within Atlantis of master priests and priestesses, and with each new generation some are selected to carry on this ascended priest role. I noticed Aigle, being the youngest of five boys and four girls, got a lot of attention from her nine older siblings. The children in order of age are sons Antonio, Achilles and Caedmon, daughters Faehim and Ianthye, then son Ichabod, daughter Laidonna, son Padraig and daughter Taavetti. As I said, all children are assessed for their gifts and abilities and Caedmon, Laidonna and Taavetti had been chosen for the Temple of light to be priests and priestesses. The other siblings would marry and find status among the Atlanteans, overseeing the land and healing of their people.

The home they lived in was attached to the Temple of Light and was a beautiful stone structure of living space and resting areas. The Light Temple was a pyramid shape with extensions that terraced out in geometric shapes in layers, and their home was attached to one of the lower terraced garden areas for easy access to the Temple, reflecting their status. Their home was quite an amazing sight, decorated with precious metals and gems from the Earth world and some of their own incarnated worlds. Creativity and art was encouraged among the people and I could see this reflected in all the people's homes and the Temples. Outside, there was beautifully kept landscaped gardens and free flowing water into pools and fountains. Cleanliness was very important to the Atlanteans to keep well and purified, which had led to the creation of both communal and private bathing areas in their homes and garden spaces.

I had been observing Aigle's daily routine in her early Earth days, some days her mother would be with her and some of the younger siblings; on others, it was the Temple nursery that oversaw the care of the younger children. Aigle was entertained by everything around her, and stimulated by music, toys and other young children. Her elders observed her closely as she was showing signs of being different from her siblings and other children. She was now nine months old and was sitting up, crawling and making language sounds. She was an observer of all around her and only had to be shown once how to do something. The elders sensed her empathic force and deep spiritual connection. She was easily soothed by the beautiful Atlantean music and attracted to all things connected to the nature energy. She adored the animals that were in her home and I sensed she understood much beyond her young age.

As I had not incarnated before into a human being, I had nothing to compare my experience against, apart from recorded transmissions like this one from other beings. My reflection of self would be influencing this in this human's Earth path, but her genetic DNA was already on a high-ascended level, with her attunement into her world and beyond. I could see the other children of a similar age did not seem to have the same intelligence and high energy in their auras.

I often converse with Avielil and the others overseeing the mission to get their feedback on my observations. They too could see a very spiritual child developing. It was felt her strength and insight was going to be needed in Atlantis to help keep this experiment on track. I was told they were working hard to keep the Atlantis energy high to prevent the lower energy from continuing to spread. A way of doing this is ensuring new babies were fully open to source at birth, so that any negative energy will not affect their development on the spiritual path. I took from this that Aigle, reflection of self and me as a combined unit had a destiny to fulfill of great importance not yet revealed to me. I am sure this will unfold as her life develops.

Life Journal – transmission 32 -
'The light within Atlantis'

It was wonderful this light day to witness Aigle at her celebration of life ceremony, where there were many gifts presented to her, one being her birth crystal. This is one Earth year on from her birth – all Atlanteans celebrate their year milestones throughout their lives. Aigle was given a crystal from our home planet from the twelve Celestial Guardians. They chose the Teycurian crystal from Durcrat, which comes from the Tesenieon Mountains. It is a light crystal, which absorbs the rays of the light star; when the energy is right, it projects the most amazing light show, creating wonderful patterns and colours. When she is old enough she will understand the significance of this birth gift, which will keep her connected to source light energy and us.

I have also observed that Atlanteans like to keep the link with their home worlds and gather once a year at the main Atlantean Temple of light. Every member of a family is invited; some family's souls are from various worlds or realms, but this makes no difference, as all work together in unison for the good of all. The time at the Temple is short as often there is a continual stream of people on this special day. In Aigle's lifetime, this custom had started to decline and a lot of the human individuals were losing their home world link and becoming less aware of the soul connection through the shifts in energies.

I feel observing Aigle's first year of life has been an honor. As well as observing her as an individual I can also observe the Atlantean way of life. I noticed that these people love water. They have various ways to travel, but are mainly seafarers.

Their ships are fast and technology has led to hover style boats that glide cross the seas at high speeds, allowing them to visit other cities quickly and explore the world around them. It has also enabled the Atlanteans who have shifted into the lower energies to leave Atlantis and populate other areas of Earth. Through this love of water they are all excellent swimmers – Aigle, for example, was introduced to water as a young baby. Young Earth babies have no fear and restraints so they adapt to water very quickly and can swim at an early age. As they grow their lung capacity expands with this skill and they can hold their breath for quite a while under water. Looking through Aigle's eyes, her experience is similar to my being underwater in our lake on my mountain trip with Zogica in a multidimensional state. She has no fear of water as a young being and I look forward to seeing her in the lakes and seas on Earth, and what the clear seas have to offer in wild life.

Life Journal – transmission 33 -
'The light within Atlantis'

Aigle was progressing in her Earth years; she was now three years old and her psychic gifts were obvious to everyone. All human Atlanteans had psychic abilities and were honoured and respected for them. The priests and priestesses were trained to a high level in these powerful energies by the Celestial Guardians. Much to her parents' delight, Aigle was to be trained to be a priestess in the Temple, which was to begin now, even though she was so young. They would often wait until a child was twelve, but they felt Aigle had achieved greater maturity for her years. She was already telepathic and had clairvoyance connecting her with the fifth dimension. I was amazed at the questions she asked, which helped her understand what she was experiencing and seeing. She knew about her soul and sensed already she had a higher self. A lot of her knowledge had not been instructed – she just knew. I felt she was going to be very insightful and wise as she grew up.

I discovered through her senses that Aigle could see auras around all living things; they fascinated her when she was younger. It was fun watching her little hands going out to them, trying to touch the colours she could see. Even at the age of three she now had an understanding of them and as she grows, she will read all living things with this gift. When a psychic can read and fully understand auras, there is nothing that the living being can hide from the psychic. They can see the being's body, history, thoughts, fears, future hopes and true feelings. I did have a slight concern that with some humans we saw auras that were darker energies – some even had black patches and there were a few that seemed to not generate an aura. We concluded for now that we were perhaps not interpreting correctly what we were seeing through Aigle's senses, and in time it would be clearer.

Aigle is an affectionate child, always giving spontaneous hugs to those around her, although as she's grown, we've noticed she is wary of one or two people. One is a priest call Guildan, who is very close to the family but not a blood relative. My reflection of self often transmits her feelings about him, which indicate she senses something different about him which makes her uneasy in his presence. The other person is a lady called Irinea, who helps her mother in the home and gives Aigle the same feelings; I observed both these people watching Aigle from a distance, and if they thought someone had noticed they would look away. It was an uneasy energy, different to the materialistic ego energy that some Atlanteans now had. We see no aura with this man or woman through her eyes, which might explain why she feels uneasy around them!

Once I realised the Atlantean experiment was wavering, I started to observe this so I could include it in my transmissions. In the first few hundred years of the fifth experiment they created a utopia on Earth. The humans all took responsibility for personal development, they were caring and sharing and their qualities were nurtured for true self and the good of all. The high priests and priestesses who oversaw the Temples were revered and loved for their selfless integrity, working alongside the twelve Celestial Guardians of Atlantis for the good of all. They set the example that nothing was done for personal gain. They thrived on the happy energy of love, kindness and helping others.

The time I have incarnated into has changed from this early Atlantis; there is now more hierarchy among the communities, some thinking they are better than others. Some have sought wealth for self and this has created the start of the fear and karma energies returning. This has caused friction among the communities as they see others as a threat to their wealth and stature. These people were and are being cast out of the cities and asked to leave to live their lives of greed elsewhere. It might not seem a very loving way to behave, but the high-ascended Atlanteans are trying to protect their future. But this went against their built-in behaviour patterns, so it was affecting their energies. By this time those cast out had built their own town communities with leaders and laws of rule. I could see and hear from adult conversation that the Atlanteans feared these people and were afraid they would try to come and disrupt their society. So now, the utopian society is no longer in clear divine pure source energy, they now have the energy of fear and doubt and this is starting to block their clear connections with the higher source.

Realising all this, I could see why Aigle and other children like her were a light among the darkness for the Atlantean people. But I also realsied she could be in danger, as the Atlanteans who have now found the darker lower energies of being would see this bright light of source as a threat. She would see right through them if they try to live among the Utopian Atlanteans as spies, attempting to gain more wealth and secrets of the Temples. The humans who had been asked to leave would notice very quickly their powers were growing weaker and their health was not as good. Their clarity of thinking would become fogged, and they would lose sight of their beginnings and early insights of existence.

I did ask the question of my mission team, that if this Atlantis experiment is faltering, would they let it carry on like the others had, or put a stop to it? I also expressed how quickly this experiment had started to fail compared to the other four. I was surprised at the silence that greeted my questions, and then Telcarian, carefully picking his thoughts, answered. He said the overseers and Intergalactic Council were aware of all within Atlantis. The way forward was under discussion, and at the moment they are working closely with the Salcaritons and the twelve Celestial Guardians for guidance and direction. They asked me not to let my feelings and this information cloud my energy and not to reveal it to any other being.

Life Journal – transmission 34 -
'The light within Atlantis'

I have mentioned a few times to you the Twelve Celestial Guardians of Atlantis so I thought I would add some knowledge here to help you with the understanding of these beautiful beings.

These beings come to Atlantis with no names, as they are recognised by their frequency and the divine chosen energy and teachings they each bring with them. They resonate on such a high pure love frequency that lower energy beings will see them as bright light forms, with each varying in colour depending on their purpose. The energy is so strong they can be seen as wispy bits of energy as they move. To me, they look like wings that beat behind them as they vibrate their amazing energy. They communicate mind to mind in the light and harmonic sound frequency and desired language that is required. They have the power to be in thousands of places and minds at once, always giving and receiving whatever is needed for the species they are helping.

They select those to whom they choose to reveal themselves. It is generally beings on a high ascension path, such as the priests and priestesses of Atlantis. They are connected to the divine source of the twelfth dimension and beyond – they have made us aware of a further spectrum of dimensions that resonates beyond the twelfth. They explain them as a reflection of the twelve, emanating from the source through a space gateway created in the womb of the universe. These next dimensions are creating further universes that are on even higher levels of light and sound frequencies. The Twelve are exploring these to see what possibilities can be created from such high source energy.

For the purpose of my updates, I have simply named them for you from my human Earth connection and understanding of them.

One - Light of Communication; Colour: astral blue ray: This light being's purpose is to oversee the incarnated souls, from selection until they return home to source; it also oversees the communication between the physical body, Earth and the celestial cosmos matrix. This is to ensure the psychic, intuitive gifts of telepathy, teleportation and telekinesis can create the required reality between the human and divine source, Earth, her star system and the galaxy. The link of good communication uses the divine light source and harmonic sound to create the energy frequency for balance that helps the flow of energy. This light being will also come to the aid of all Atlanteans when requested to do so, to give healing on a higher energy level. This helps the human to help them transform negative energy into positive energy, to ensure no fear; doubt and karma energy can seep in. It also helps to teach how to shift consciousness to a new way of being, bringing new attitudes to self-healing and a positive way to look at their individual lives and beyond. The human will only receive this healing if they truly wish to; the guardian can only help beings in acceptance of them. This is because it opens the mind channel for the guardian's love, healing and teachings.

Two - Light of Grace Within; Colour: fire red ray: This light being's purpose is to sustain the warrior of sacred courage to ensure peace within, inspiring Atlanteans to accept change that comes to them in grace, and bringing inner power of strength, stamina and purpose to live a true spiritual path.

Through all changes comes friendships, hope and integrity; this warrior energy ensures the human being has the strongest and balanced energy to make the best of all new experiences and relationships. This also extends to the balance of the Earth energies and to tame fear rising from unforeseen Earth energies, like thunder and lighting. The warrior is the inner strength needed to ensure the peace and balance of all to sustain the power needed of a higher energy way of being for the whole.

Three – Light of Connection; Colour: star yellow ray: This light being is connected with the crown chakra, ensuring the connection of the incarnated soul is sustained with the higher self. One of its purposes is to teach us how to control our emotions and find bliss away from the darker aspects of our emotions, which will liberate us from lower energies. This being also brings wisdom, helping the Atlanteans to be wise, developing creative thoughts to bring new ideas and enchantment to their lives, and improve their way of being.

Four – Light of Teaching; Colour: translucent ray: This light being is the divine source teacher; leading the way that Atlanteans need to stay true to the spiritual divine path. The Temple of Teachers holds quartz crystals called light guides, where the required teachings are downloaded from the divine knowledge library records. The teachings given to selected human teachers include wisdom, philosophy, arts, music, drama and dance. The teachings are levelled at children to bring an advanced understanding of their purpose and powers – how to stay balanced and use their powers such as telepathic, telekinetic and psychic for the good of all.

Five – Light of Truth; Colour: violet ray: This light being is the guidance that leads us away from karma energy, self-inflicted doubt and negative feelings. It brings wisdom, love, transformation and all truths, helping humans align with their incarnated soul and the divine source. This being's light energy is to give strength and protection for the life journey on Earth, channeling its light through the upper chakras when requested. This light connection keeps the humans linked with their incarnated souls and the upper source energy of love. This being is like a pillar of inner strength and can be called upon through a meditation state of consciousness when required.

Six – Light of Healing; Colour: emerald ray: This light being is the healer of humanity, and the link between Earth and the creative source energy of the overseers. Part of this role is to bring healing to help keep the humans attuned to Earth and the universe, adjusting the humanoid frequencies when called upon. This being's healing force comes in through the heart chakra, bringing physical and mind balance as the healing energy brings relaxation and calm, leading to harmony. Its connection runs deep with the energy of Mother Earth and the human form and helps the human form return to the Earth's energy on completion of the physical life. The incarnated soul is then released and this being helps to bring them, with their guides, back through the cosmic light matrix and communication to its home source of origin.

Seven – Light of Knowledge; Colour: indigo ray: This light being is the doorway to knowledge, wisdom and resolving the mysteries of the Earth plane through the halls of truth. He guides the humans to the energy of the Earth, building Temples on ley lines in the three dimensional matrix to help build Earth's energies and keep her balanced. It also oversees the elemental energies connected to the Earth and helps humans to connect with and respect Mother Earth and stay connected to their divine energy. This being also brings clear vision or clarity to the mind through meditation, so the telepathic process can bring in learning and communication.

Eight – Light of Energy; Colour: amber ray: This light being is the overseer of Earth's energy and is linked with the Earth chakra. As described in my chakra information earlier in the transmissions, the Earth chakra keeps the human grounded to their planet. This is key, as they are vibrating in the higher love energy with their incarnated soul and life connection to the higher love source. This being also makes sure the human is guided to respect their planet and ensures they attune to the frequency of their plants and animals, all living in unison. It oversees Earth's ascension and helps mould what she is; it also monitors the energy by filtering out any negative influences that go out from Mother Earth into the universe.

Nine – Light of Order; Colour: lilac ray: This light being is the overseer of the twelve principle laws of the universe. It will guide the teacher on Earth to bring these principles of truth into their teachings. If acted upon, the laws bring balanced order to their Earthly and spiritual physical existence. Making sure the human understands the law will help them move forward on their correct path, guiding them towards love and away from despair. This being also ensures the connection of the spiritual truth that each Atlantean is aware of deep inside, so their purpose of incarnation is not forgotten.

Ten – Light of Presence; Colour: pink ray: This light being helps the human form to work on self presence, with the guidance of unconditional love leading to an open heart of giving. It guides the human's destiny so they are a friendly companion to others, using calmness, empathy, and kindness for the good of the collective society. This being works with the crown and heart chakras energy, ensuring the connection to the divine light source and the human form to understand the importance of this.

Eleven: Light of Comfort; Colour: azure ray: This light being brings the essence of comfort that gives strength to the human life with abundance of love. This essence of energy brings compassion, empathy, non-judgemental thoughts, patience, kindness, forgiveness, gratitude and sincerity. Once the human has a balance of these comforting energies they will have clarity of mind and intelligence of the way forward. It has a strong connection with the heart chakra, as the comfort essence helps to soften the energy from the human with the connection to the divine.

Twelve – Light of Love; Colour: silver ray: This light being is from the divine feminine energy of creation and links us all in the silver ray of love that passes through everything in the universe and twelve dimensions. This being ensures the teachings of true compassion, as no human being should ever feel alone. It also encourages compassion, romance and true love, bringing the internal flame of twin souls together for reunion on the Earth plane. The Atlanteans see the union of love as a sacred act and nurture their children to understand this love and compassion from the divine source.

As I said in an earlier transmission, these beings have a star ship that is in the Earth's atmosphere above the Light Temple of Atlantis. They are highly evolved light beings, all connected with various home planets and realms of those that are reincarnating. They work closely with the Salcaritons, helping the incarnated worlds they are involved with; it was they who that suggested they helped with this fifth experiment. The star ship is designed to be a Temple of Light of unconditional love for teaching and knowledge for the Atlantean people. The role of these twelve cosmic beings is to oversee the experiment then report back any findings to the Intergalactic Council and the overseers.

The star ship also has another vital role; it has a Calentian crystal that powers the Atlantis biosphere dome. It is also a computer that records everything – a library of knowledge on Atlantis and all of its history. The Temple of Light in central Atlantis has a smaller Calentian crystal that is connected with the higher star ship crystal. The other eleven Temples in the other Atlantean cities spread across the lands also have crystals, all of which link to the main Atlantean Light Temple crystal. Each Celestial Guardian is connected with a Temple, linking with the priests and priestesses to guide the people.

Life Journal – transmission 35 -
'The light within Atlantis'

This light day has bought great excitement for me as I visited the finished Alcerian Touliza Creatorion designed and overseen by Zogica. As promised, Telcarian arranged this at an appropriate moment, planning a light day of exclusive invitations for off-world dignitaries involved in the Atlantis mission.

The Creatorion was built near our main city with its own biosphere dome, set on the shores of a beautiful underground lake. It is a very big complex, lit by a mixture of light starlight, the fluorescent crystals and the smooth domed rocks that cover the lake, and crystal energy lights. The outdoor animal and plant life is unique to these underground growing conditions and does not occur on the planet's surface.

We all arrived in various ways at the Creatorion; I chose to travel with Zogica and my parents in our crystal craft, while others chose to arrive at various teleportation stations throughout the complex. We all assembled in the great hall, which was a marvel of crystal structures carved with historical episodes and elements of our planet. Scattered in this huge space were fountains of flowing energy liquid, with crystals that slowly changed colours, creating a very tranquil mood. Seating was placed around these areas for all to relax and admire the beauty of this structure, which is a piece of art in itself. This is also a space that can be used for the performance arts of music, movement and voice.

Just off the great hall are various chambers for art displays, some of which have been commissioned from other off-world species we have visited and befriended. We spent quite a while admiring these various works of art. My favourite was some statues of movement and dance from an artist on our planet. They moved to orchestrated music and interacted with us as we approached the display, and were marvelous to see.

After refreshments we ventured outside to the beautiful tiered gardens that fell away to the underground lake and outdoor amphitheatre. The amphitheatre was especially designed for acoustics of sound to enhance the live performances. The gardens are designed like living rooms, each space having its own design and planting styles. Among these spaces were areas to sit and admire the gardens and the art that was displayed outside.

I felt no one was disappointed with this beautiful place and I was very proud when Zogica stood up to do a closing speech about the design, thanking everyone for their support and kind thoughts.

I am now back in my chambers after checking in with my reflection of self, relaxing with Zogica and Dolso and reflecting on this wonderful light day. Everything feels calm and just right in my world.

Life Journal – transmission 36 -
'The light within Atlantis'

My light days have passed so quickly, blending into a combination of self-care for my energies, connecting to my reflective self with Aigle, and catching up with my mission team. I am also trying to balance my time with Dolso and family. I have noticed Dolso has slowed down a bit in his bouncy ways and is a calmer now as he ages, I suppose maturing is the word that reflects this energy transition in him. He has so much love to give everyone he meets and you can only smile when he's around you.

I have also been looking at my own future plans and have decided to help my mother with the meditation and multidimensional training. My plan is to train at designated moments and then support her in this role in the future. My scientific interests and experiences from the incarnation process lend themselves well to this natural progression for me.

I am also delighted to say Aigle is growing into a beautiful child; at the human age of five she has long wavy auburn hair with a light tanned skin. Her eyes are clear blue, reminding you of the aqua marine stones found on Earth. She has a lovely nature with nothing but kindness and love for all around her. She is very connected to the high source of love and light and her abilities are going beyond what has been expected of her. I have been fascinated in her art, as she has painted our home world, already understanding she is connected to another place. She has great visionary skills and an insightful mind. I do feel a very strong connection to this young being, I know her as I would know a very good friend. But I also know her on a deeper level of mind and body, feeling everything she feels and seeing everything she sees.

She has a very curious mind and analyses all she sees and feels. She makes quick decisions based on her emotions, a great inner knowing connecting to the higher source. Her telepathic mind connection is nearly fully developed and she has astounded her elders, as she is already capable of telekinesis. She often uses her telekinesis skill during play, moving small crystals in geometric formations in the air to entertain the other children. I have discovered over the Earth time that quite a few Atlanteans are losing these highly developed skills as they connect more and more to the lower self energies and begin to lose the high link connection to the power source that gives these skills.

This is not something we are not yet capable of on Diacurat, but Ioliismiem said we could learn to connect to the object we wish to move by learning the right frequency. This would be a combination of the frequency of the object, the intent of mind frequency, and the energy of space around you to achieve this, all combining to a unique frequency to control the objects you wish to move. I am going to have a chat with my mother about this and see what her thoughts are on us developing this skill; we would only acquire this gift if it could be of positive use to us in some way.

Aigle's home life has altered around her over the last couple of Earth years, as her three older brothers have left the home environment and gone out into Atlantis or other cities. There has been some tension, as the eldest brother Antonio has been drawn into the materialistic energy and is seeking power over his fellow humans. He was advised to leave the home to seek this as her parents wanted to protect the remaining siblings from this energy. A lot of this they thought was hidden from Aigle, but she is well aware when things are unbalanced within the home, and it saddened her to see the spaces emerging at the family table as her brothers slowly left for whatever reason.

Saying all this, I feel I am not seeing an Earth child experience a true childhood, as Aigle does play with children of her age, but she's often apart, watching or being instructed by her teachers from the Temple. The Celestial Guardians are intrigued with her, and observe her development from afar, as they do with all the children under their instruction. There will be a point at which she will engage with them but they wish this to be when she is older, and has even greater understanding. This would then help her understand what they will reveal to her of their powers and knowledge.

Life Journal – transmission 37 –
'The light within Atlantis'

My reflective self has been taking the opportunity to leave Aigle's body when she is sleeping to travel the Earth, exploring the beauty she beholds. But we have had to be careful, as Aigle is becoming aware of this, because the out of body travels can be remembered by those in the higher source connection energies as dreams. When the time is right, she will eventually understand this connection with her incarnated soul and communicate with my reflective self to jointly travel at will in the dream state of the fourth dimension, and remember her travels. I should explain that my reflective self is not of her own mind, it is connected to mine. I will trigger these out of body experiences, to keep the higher self-connection link and Aigle's inner soul safe.

This journey I am taking as an incarnated soul is one of wonder. I realise I have been placed in a human with a high source connection, and the Atlantean people see her as a sign of hope as others fall away from their utopian society. The Intergalactic Council is also trying to raise the experiment's energies with the newborns, as they have not given up hope. I am wondering this light day what it would be like to be incarnated into a child that has a more normal life in Atlantis. Perhaps if Diacurat decides this path of incarnation is for us I will find out one day in Earth's future

As it stands at the moment in Aigle's time, Earth is a beautiful planet. The northern areas that were the last to come out of the ice age are now flourishing as nature reclaims the land. It is wonderful to see the purified lands, mountains and water – this planet is a blue jewel in the cosmos due to its high water content. The animal species of the oceans and lands vary around the planet, from large roaming mammals to the tiny mouse and flying creatures and various insects. The animals and nature support the ecosystem of Earth. The weather patterns stay stable due to the biosphere protection around it. Earth reminds me of Diacurat, with its high mountains and lakes, although the mineral structure is different. I also love the vast plains with their abundance of wild flowers.

I have realised that Diacurat would be defined more as a crystalline rock structure, which is a great energy conductor and intelligence of its own. Our plant life is different, as the cellular structure creates a different texture and appearance. The Diacurat plant life shimmers, visually vibrating and moving with the energy around them. For example, if I hold my hand out to a flower, the flower will move away from me, observe and then move back towards my energy. On Earth, the plants create the chemicals for the atmosphere needed to sustain life. On Diacurat, we do not rely just on the air source for survival, we thrive from the energy around us and the balance of light star energy. This is hard to translate for you, but if I visited Earth in my physical form I would need a survival suit with the balance of our climate for me to live. But if I multidimensional travel to Earth no air is needed; I can survive in the atmosphere as my multidimensional body draws on the love energy of the planet and beyond to survive.

The animals brought to Earth to raise her vibrations are thriving. They include various land, sky and water mammals. I do have my favourites, I have to admit. I love the large land mammal species I know as Menbal. They have a long trunk, large ears and are so family orientated, a warrior as in the strength of nature, but with the deepest wisdom and spiritual awareness. They also have what is translated as a flying horse; similar to the ones on our planet, they run the plains and also choose to let humans ride them. My next favourite is the water creature I know as Delphinsirius who came from the Sirius region of the universe, with beautiful harmonious feelings and great intelligence. They were brought to Earth due to their intelligence and high frequency connection to all around them and the divine source. I also adore the butterflies of Earth's world; they have majestic colours and patterns, and are a symbol of transformation for the Atlanteans. It is hoped these animals and many others that came to Earth would help balance the energies of the planet, helping to aid the success of the experiment. This happened in the early days, but was not enough to sustain the high-energy frequency. Other factors were needed to help support this, the main one being all humans staying in the high state of love energy connection without any thought of self.

The one thing we do continue to notice with Aigle is her diversion from certain humans. She has not yet discussed this with her elders, but we see all and feel this within her. She sees the energy of all living things, and it's as if she's seeing darkness within the light of these beings, which affects her trust in them. My mission team has discussed this and felt she might be picking up on the lower ego energy that is starting to swamp the experiment. But there is another thought that she is picking up, a frequency none of us can see or feel as yet – all will become clear in the future when she is older and more attuned to her world.

Life Journal – transmission 38 -
'The light within Atlantis'

This is a transmission I always hoped to make, and I am so grateful to be making it this light day. I had been observing Aigle and as I came out of my mission chamber, there was a lot of excitement and some wonderful news relayed to me. Remember I told you about my brother Alechoian and his star ship disappearing while on a mission? This light day brings the news that his star ship has been found! When the ship disappeared we no longer felt his life force, but we never gave up hope that an unexplained event occurred to take his star ship and crew out of our reach.

My parents have spoken to him through a transmission link, and he will be back in a few light days. Alechoian's star ship is at a star station port way having repairs carried out before he can make the trip home.

Alechoian explained to my parents that there was a fold in the fabric energy of the dimension of the universe they were travelling through. These often show up as an energy spiral funnel that can distort the fabric of the geometric structure of space. We know where most of them are in the universe delta, but due to an unseen light star energy burst that had distorted the area they were in, they were caught off-guard. They had little time to pull away from the gravity created by the energy funnel and got caught up in it and its distorted energy waves pulled them into another dimension in another universe.

The fabric of space and energy changes in the different dimensions. In the third dimension, for example, the energy space stays quite flat and free flowing, but is a lower heavier energy. The rolling existence of time exists in this three-dimensional layer. As you ascend into the fourth and fifth dimensions the energy space becomes lighter, and can curve and bend with more flexibility. Beings exist in this lighter state without time restraints. As you progress into the sixth, seventh, eighth and ninth dimensions, beings can adapt the energy of the universe to travel through light way portholes to far off destinations, arriving in the moment they left their starting point in their reality. The higher tenth, eleventh and twelfth dimensions can create all physical and ethereal energy for all dimensions, placing through the cosmic matrix layers where they need to be to start the creation of life.

Alechoian also explained they found themselves in a new dimension and were unsure of their whereabouts within the Universe Delta, but they soon realised that nothing matched their star charts. They checked their data banks and found the information they were seeking. Luckily, the high-ascended beings of the twelfth dimensions had opened a gateway to this universe to explore its possibilities. They found the coordinates of the gateway and made their way to it. They were spotted by the overseers and brought through the gateway and led back to the ninth dimension for repairs, and soon they will be taken on their homeward journey. The overseers have now placed a star gate on the spiral energy funnel that took them through to monitor the tear in the fabric of the cosmic energy matrix. This is because these funnels can alter and shut without notice or get bigger, so it's a safety measure for other starships.

I am delighted that I can also feel Alechoian's life force again, and it's so wonderful to know I will see him again soon.

Life Journal – transmission 39 –
of 'The light within Atlantis'

With the excitement over for now at the pending return of Alechoian, I will update you on Aigle's progress in Atlantis. Her family life has stayed balanced under the protection of her parents and priest guardians. As she approaches her eighth Earth year she is excelling in her studies and development. But I must also not forget to enlighten you about the normal human behaviour I witness every light day with her. Like us, there is a daily routine, starting on awakening with cleansing the body and eating. She has individual space responsibility by keeping her resting chamber tidy. She studies in the morning when it's cooler and the afternoon is leisure time with friends and family. In the evening, the family endeavours to eat together, reflecting on their day and all contributing to the conversation. It is a community-based society, and Aigle's family and Temple members give healing to the community and in return receive food to meet all their needs. If a member of the utopian society is unable to contribute they are looked after until their Earth life ends. Sadly though, we are witnessing through the materialistic ego greed that has entered this experiment, that some humans are suffering, and being allowed to, by their fellow humans.

With the human children like Aigle still in the higher ascended energy, there are no tears or fear, but only laughter. But I have noticed in Atlantis, where the human children are in the families heading into the lower energy, that tears, tantrums and fear are starting to show more and more. Aigle, I realised, is quite cocooned in her environment, not witnessing any of the lower energy behaviour at the moment.

She adores nature, and with her teacher's guidance, soon realised this helped keep herself balanced – remember the Earth chakra. She loves to walk in the woods and sit against an old tree, feeling its wisdom. It was fascinating to be with her when she linked into the energy of the tree and listened to the ancient wisdom of the land. She has also learnt to dance and play around trees, helping with the equilibrium of the energies. The land used to be a rich, fertile, abundant source creating richly flavoured foods, but since the experiment has started to waver the lands are not as fertile. When all is in balance the plants grown in tune with the high source energies creating better yields, nourishment and flavours.

Aigle had received this information from the trees and felt saddened by the way the humans were treating this Earth she lived on. She also adores the energy of a beach where the family spend leisure time near Atlantis – the water energy is very agreeable to her. She is now allowed to swim in the sea and lakes under adult supervision. I adore this when she does as I get a wonderful perspective of life under the Earth's oceans and natural waterways.

Her foresight is way beyond her years and I find she relates more to adults than children of her own age. I sometimes find myself wishing she could just play innocently, without feeling and sensing all around her. But this was not her path; her path is to be a priestess and to bring enlightenment to others.

Her close human world had no materialistic desires or need for power over others and lived in a balanced, harmonious energy. She spent her time with other family members and close friends following creative pursuits when not in lessons, and her favourites were painting and music. Aigle has a wonderful singing voice as well that can mesmerise you. Everyone stops to listen when she sings; she often sings to herself as if she is lost in her own little world.

Aigle might have appeared sometimes to be in her own world but she did not miss anything and her hearing was acute. A recent conversation was the topic of my mission team meeting this light day. It was between her father and other senior members from other Temples. Some of the cities had started to show advanced decline in the balance energies and there had even been cases of violence among the citizens. This was quite a worrying occurrence and the lower energies were starting to affect everyone – including crops and nature's energies. They decided to take this to the Intergalactic Council for deliberation.

Meanwhile I was just to carry on as I am on my life incarnation's path, learning as much as I can from this young human.

Life Journal – transmission 40 –
'The light within Atlantis'

I have just come back from catching up with my brother Alechoian in my mother's Temple chambers. There has been so much excitement since his return home, I have not really had a chance to be alone with him. As well as family and friends wanting to embrace his energy and smile, the ascended science masters wanted to talk to him about his experiences, so he has been kept very busy.

This light day brought the solitude we needed with each other. He is older than me by five hyons and has always been my protector, confidant and close friend. I did find it hard at first when he left our safe home environment and went out into our world and beyond. But as I grew up I realised he was fulfilling his destiny and dreams, as we all should, and was pleased for him. It took all my strength to stay focused when I no longer felt his physical life force. I had to trust all would be well and one day, if the universe was willing, he would return to us. For me, it was not knowing whether he had died or was lost that I struggled with.

But I don't have to dwell on this anymore, or hold it in my heart. I had to laugh this light day as he's already planning his next mission and now wants to explore unchartered space. He has applied to the intergalactic master sciences for this role. They work with the overseers and their gateways to explore other universes, using special star ships to explore and charter the stars. This was how Alechoian's star ship managed to trace its way home.

Alechoian was very pleased at the news of the bonding promise between Zogica and me. He has known Zogica all his life and treated him like a younger brother. His disappearance had affected Zogica too, but it had a positive effect, making him more determined to do well and lived a full life that would make Alechoian proud.

Dolso also took to Alechoian straightaway and flopped all over him for a loving petting. Poor Dolso had seemed a bit unwell lately, so he has been to the healing rooms with me and has perked up a lot since then. His species does not live many hyons - he is ageing now, so I have to be prepared for health setbacks. But today he is very happy, bouncing around as he usually does. He always brightens up my day and brings cheer to many others too.

I am happy to transmit that my family feels whole again bringing a new balance to us all; I had not realised just how much my brothers disappearance had affected our inner energies.

Life Journal – transmission 41 –
'The light within Atlantis'

I have realised that I have not explained the time frame of Earth life in relation to time on Diacurat, and how this affects my viewing of Aigle's existence, which is at the moment happening far across the universe from me. I did explain in a earlier transmission the length of lights days varied between the two planets. Her life is not running along beside mine, moment for moment, because it is in a different reality and dimension. Every light day, I choose to view her journey with my reflective self, but when she has lived several of her Earth months, I can scroll back and forth to view her life up to the point where her time coincides with mine – but no further. On this light day, for example, I cannot go beyond her twelfth year, as she has not yet lived beyond this point in her reality, and my reflective self is restricted from seeing the future of her existence as we want to capture her life and feelings without knowing the outcome. If I wished, I could, with a highly ascended being like Telcarian, move forward to view a future path, but because this could be altered at any time by events on Atlantis, it could create a false future impression. So we let Aigle's existence live out its course of time in her reality. The highly ascended masters and other beings can be part of an existence that has already taken place, placing themselves in that reality to observe, moving back and forth as they please in that chosen time frame. I hope this has translated well for you, as it is not an easy subject to explain.

I have created this transmission in Aigle's twelfth Earth year, as this is a time of great transition for her. The last four years have been a continuous cycle of home life and Temple teachings and Aigle being protected by her elders. Her rite of passage into womanhood has started with what humans call her first menstruation. A true sign of a woman's fertility, when the eggs of life are released and if not impregnated by the male of the species, the body discards them. I noticed there was some mild pain with this and Aigle felt uncomfortable and restricted. Her mother and sisters had prepared her for this moment of transition, but it took her by surprise on the day it started and she thought it would take a bit of getting used to. I also noticed it affected her energy balance but she will soon adjust to it with time. Aigle's future was to be without marriage and she would remain celibate; her sexual energies would redefine to raise her energies for higher communication with the divine source. This was, I discovered, to be a pivotal year for her, as she would now be initiated into the priesthood of light in Atlantis.

This would involve a high status ceremony, and she would move into the Temple full time for her development to be enhanced. I could feel she was excited but was also a little sad and unsure about leaving her home. All her brothers and sisters had left home by now and her brother Caedmon and sisters Laidonna and Taavetti had already been initiated into the Temple's priesthood. I was confident from what I knew of Aigle's personality that she would adapt easily to the new changes and challenges ahead of her.

The Temple's elders and twelve Celestial Guardians were really looking forward to this new phase and hoped her shining light would raise the energies of the Atlantis Temple. There was a lot of hope in this child prodigy, and that her elevated energies combined with other new arrivals would bring new hope to the Atlantis experiment. I know Aigle was aware of this and she chose to take it all in her stride and not feel pressured by the heavier weight of expectancy that lay on her shoulders. At times like this I would send her healing energy through my reflective self, to help support and keep her strong.

Life Journal – transmission 42 -
'The light within Atlantis'

This is my toughest transmission yet as this recent event has really shaken my energies. My dearest friend Dolso passed away this dark night. He had being showing signs of his old age and my mother and me had been giving him healing that helped for a while. The ascended master healers even tried to help me, but sometimes old age cannot be reversed. I noticed yesterday he was not eating and did not want to play, his eyes looked so tired and his coat had lost its shimmer, as if his life force was fading. I took the decision to stay with him and not connect to my reflective self and I am glad I did. He slowly got weaker through the day; my mother came to be with me as well, as she sensed as I had he was going to pass over. I lay with him on cushions with his head on my lap. I was stroking his head and telling him how much I loved him and it was OK to leave me, even though my heart was breaking. We were giving him healing energy for the transition of life he was about to take and in the early moments of darkness he took his last breath. I felt his spirit leave, and could see his spirit energy pause, as if he took one look back at me to say thank you – and then his energy soared high and was gone.

He will travel back to the dimensions of elemental creation to be with his spirit group of existence and be his old self once again. I knew bringing him here would enhance my energies because of the love we found with each other, and I had not realised how much his loss would affect me. As a species we have long life and as yet, I have not lost many in my lifetime. I need to quickly deal with this experience and rebalance for the sake of the mission. Avielil came to help me; we took Dolso's physical form to the cremation chamber in the Temple and with a small ceremony he was turned to ashes. I then chose his favourite place in the Temple gardens and scattered them, knowing he would have appreciated this gesture.

I know he's out of pain and his spirit is now running free in the elemental planes. Avielil assured me that with our strong connection, one day we would find each other again. His knowledge of incarnation and energies is quite vast. He believes when you have had a strong unconditional love bond as we had, our spirit energies will be drawn together again in a future moment. I might not recognise it as Dolso, but will know we have been together before and the connection will be very strong. Depending on their ascension level, ethereal elemental energies can ask to reincarnate with the same family, to bring them love and balance.

Later in this light day Zogica came to see me, I held him tight for a long time and I felt calm and recharged. He understood how I felt without any words and thoughts needed. I also had to remember Dolso touched many hearts and would be missed by many, and his love will always be with us in our hearts and minds.

Life Journal – transmission 43 -
'The light within Atlantis'

Things have settled down after the passing of Dolso, I have stopped looking for him now when I return to my chambers and can smile at my memories of him without my energies being disrupted, although it did take me a couple of light days longer than expected to achieve this. Avielil and the others were fine about it, monitoring my link to my reflective self and Aigle to make sure it stayed strong. It remained stable but they thought it was best I linked back into them when I was one hundred per cent settled again. Because I am still in physical form and our species still has not fully managed to control all emotions, this loss has been a real test of my energies and self-control.

I have had to learn to put any loss and sadness to the side so I can always be the best for the whole. Other species who have achieved this would then choose the right time to release these emotions, so you keep the loving memories without the negative emotional feelings, always staying on the love vibration.

I appreciate life around me is going well, and my mother and father are well and working hard at the Temple in their individual roles. My brother is due to leave soon as he was accepted by the master scientists to join the science corps and will be off again, exploring the universes. I look forward to his transmissions, updating us on his travels. Zogica is also very well; the Creatorion project has opened lots of new avenues for him to explore. He and his team have been asked by some off-world planets to visit and advise on design and building methods, which is quite an honour. He is also going to look at new methods to improve our own planet's structures for healing, mainly looking at crystal materials that will help enhance this, so he is going to be kept very busy.

I had advised Zogica on the crystal pyramids being used in Atlantis, explaining that they are placed on the planet's energy lines to enhance the higher energy connections. A large volume of magnetic concentration exists within the pyramidal boundaries, which helps protect the humans from the adverse effects of negative energies. The pyramid will help to create a beneficial environment for healing, helping the physical body to function properly.

I had found out that the twelve Temples of Atlantis were all on ley energy lines, resonating with the Earth's magnetic field, which creates life force energy. They were also aligned with the magnetic north of the Earth, using the stars as a link to home worlds and where light way portals are positioned. This helps to link Earth's energy with the energies of the universe and enhance the energy connection to the high ascension levels of the tenth and twelfth dimensions. All the Temples are near water such as the ocean or rivers, as this also helps with the energy connections. All the art on the Temple walls shows their history, and the constellations and stars they align with, so everyone can understand the meaning behind the Temples and those who use them. The Temples are also elevated high above their city and are designed for the best energy retention for the whole area.

The main Atlantis city is designed on a format of circles expanding out over the land; the circles help hold the energy from the main Temple and celestial star ship, and help it ripple out evenly across the city, helping with higher source connection. Other cities had square layouts, or a mixture of both, but all have the pyramid-style Temples which include a crystal based pyramid structure purely for healing. When someone enters the pyramid it constantly tries to keep its own energy field in balance and in doing so, can help to balance and release blockages from the human energy fields such as auras and chakras.

Zogica is fascinated by the information I divulged to him and he's going to ask to explore Earth structures in Atlantis through the transmitted recordings in the universal library. I am sure this will benefit our own healing structures when he has a good understanding of how they work.

I also linked into my reflective self this light day and they were busy preparing for Aigle's initiation into the Temple which is taking place in a few light days, so I will bring that to you in a transmission soon.

Life Journal – transmission 44 -
'The light within Atlantis'

I have had a wonderful light day sharing Aigle's experiences on Earth, as she was initiated as a priestess into the Temple of Light.

The elders and Celestial Guardians had decided the time was right, because her feminine power had now been enhanced with the onset of womanhood, and her powers were so advanced they needed to be harnessed and trained to be used correctly for the good of all. I realised this was key to harnessing her powers as she was starting to feel a bit detached, trying hard to deal with bodily emotions as well as mind control, and this was affecting her balance of energies.

Aigle was prepared for her initiation by the high priestess Cardinea and her two sisters Laidonna and Taavetti. They washed her in specially prepared waters that contained herbs for purification, then rubbed her with body oils. She was clothed in a simple white dress made of two parts, designed to drape the body form; the trick was wrapping it so that it stayed in position, before being secured at the shoulder with an ornate brooch. Her hair was braided with decorative crystal beads. I thought she looked very pretty and ethereal in her innocence.

Aigle was given a breakfast of fruit and water then she was led to the domed initiation chamber. No one speaks at this time, as she is led to a throne and takes her seat. Then all the priestesses of the Temple file in and surround her. This ceremony is kept in the feminine energy, while the priest's initiations are kept in the male. This is so that their separate energies are not influenced by the opposites in this process of mind expansion. Cardinea stands in front of the throne and starts to dance and chant from the source of creation. The other priestesses join in the chant and start moving in a slow rhythm, clockwise around the throne. Gradually, the energy in the dome chamber starts to change and from above, the Celestial Guardians create the energy of a golden light that starts to fill the chamber. This light is focused on Aigle and is so pure it has the power to cleanse her of any fear and restrictions she puts on her own mind. The chanting then stops and all including Aigle wait silently in meditation until the light disperses and Aigle feels her mind clear. Cardinea knows when this has been achieved through her own powerful intuition.

This clarity of mind is the understanding that there is so much more than your own moment of existence, clearing the mind of the doubt energy to make way for the higher source inspiration energy. Cardinea then takes Aigle by the hand to the Temple's sacred pool; powerful crystals and the Celestial Guardians with the purest source of unconditional love have cleansed these waters, purifying anything they touch. Aigle is undressed and led down the steps to enter the water by Cardinea, who gently submerges her. Aigle then comes back up to the surface and swims in the waters; when she emerges from the pool she is dried by the others and dressed in her priestess robes. The robes are purple and lilac silk with silver thread decoration, creating a beautiful free-flowing gown.

As this all happened when she climbed up the steps to leave the pool, I could feel Aigle's consciousness expand. Her mind was now unrestricted, the third dimensional matrix energy was gone, and she was now a vessel to receive pure unconditional love high dimensional energies. She had the deep wisdom to accept love, the truth, the justice, and the harmony for all beings. She knew that this power had to be used wisely and that wisdom would be at the core of all her decisions and choices.

This was a pivotal moment in her life, as I now felt more connected to her than at any other time, with the connection of soul and mind made. The mission team also felt this and we all looked forward to see what happened now with her powers of connection to source.

After the ceremony her sisters took her to their chamber, which they would share with her. It was lovely that she would have this family connection in her new life. I discovered there would be a daily routine of meditation, healing and lessons for her. The elders wanted to enhance her gifts but make sure she could also understand and control them. These included telepathic communication, telekinesis, clairvoyance and her psychic ability to read others. She was already very advanced for her age and it all had been a child's journey of exploration and discovery; now I could feel the underlying seriousness of this initiation in the adult discussions about her.

The Atlantis experiment had continued to falter as more humans turned to the materialistic ego existence. The twelve Celestial guardians were working hard to try to maintain the balance within the Atlantean cities, but they were finding it very challenging. I feel there is an unseen force slowly stripping away the utopian society that has been created over the last few hundred Earth years.

Life Journal – transmission 45 -
'The light within Atlantis'

I have had a delightful light day; Zogica surprised me with a gift of a Peltoian feline. It is a youngling cat-like creature that will grow into an adult, much as an Earth kitten would grow into a cat. I was quite taken aback, as I had not even thought about another elemental being coming into my life again. She was asleep when I received her; she is silver grey and long-haired, with white tips at the end of her fur, and on her ears and paws. My heart immediately melted at this cute creature. When she woke up her purple eyes mesmerised me – they are like cut gems! She was very playful and hungry, so we fed her and had a fun time playing with her until she eventually wore herself out. We decided to name her Glitle, meaning sparkle; the name reflects her expressive eyes. I do believe she will melt many hearts, just as Dolso did.

While I am reflecting with you I am pleased to say all is well on my home world and with my family. My brother has left us again going off on his adventures on a science ship, and I reflect on the excitement in his eyes as he left to join his crew members. Before he left, he told me that he knows the discoveries they make will help future explorers follow them into the uncharted universes. I cannot even imagine what he will discover out there in the unknown, but look forward to the light day I can see the transmissions of his adventures.

My moments at the Sacred Light Council have been an amazing experience so far. My time with the Atlantis mission has led me to set my future plans with my mother's work. I know this will be the starting point of my Temple role, which will only grow as I do. I will not live in the Temple when the mission is over, I will live with Zogica in our own chambers. I am happy to say Zogica has been designing our new dwelling on some land near a lake in our home domed city Vatical. He was going to surprise me but then decided it would be better for us both to have input into the design of our home. I am glad he did ask me, as I wish to have a big meditation and calming space, while he will need his workshop space to build 3D models that demonstrate his ideas – it's more of a hobby as our technology is way beyond model building by hand for designs, and we can create models from mind connection alone. We plan to move into our new dwelling after our bonding ceremony and when we are happy with the design, he will start creating it in his own time.

Zogica is also keeping up with his multidimensional training and now goes out on his own around our planet. I have not multidimensional travelled since the mission began, as I need to be focused on my connection with my reflective self. But we both look forward to the light day when the mission is over and we can travel together again. We might not be seeing each other every light day but our bond is growing stronger and we are nurturing each other's successes as part of this growth.

Following on from my transmission that mentioned Aigle's telekinesis skills, my mother told me today that she and some other ascended masters have discovered that we are capable of this ability with some guidance and practice. They are going to master this themselves and see how it can help our people before they bring it out for training to others. They will also study other species in the universe that use this technique to move objects, and its benefits, to see what they can learn from them.

Life Journal – transmission 46 -
'The light within Atlantis'

This has been a very busy light day for me. I am just back from meeting with the mission team about my progress as an incarnated soul and the Atlantis mission as a whole. As you know we meet often and I was updating them all this light day on my viewpoint of progress. I was explaining to them that Aigle was now entering her fourteenth Earth year and the transformation since she had become a priestess is quite remarkable. What was of great interest is I have experienced my first higher self-interaction with her.

When she was initiated as a priestess her life routine altered, and her lessons started early in the day after breakfast and meditation. She was now taking teaching and guidance for five Earth days, followed by a couple of days' rest. The high priestess herself, Cardinea, had taken on this teaching role due to the advanced state of mind consciousness Aigle had reached. Cardinea and many others, including the Twelve Celestial Guardians, thought that by the time she was sixteen she would be at such an advanced level she would be of equal standing in her mind control and intuition as Cardinea herself. But it was felt that as she had been so closely guarded from the outside world, and had only been introduced to the Temple way of life for two years, she had not yet gained enough life experiences. After discussion, it was agreed that when she was sixteen, Aigle should meet the Twelve Celestial Guardians that oversee Atlantis.

Reaching the Earth age of sixteen is another milestone in human womanhood; if Aigle had not been a priestess she would have been of marrying age. They felt she would be mature enough in the human mind by then to deal with all of the transition energy that would be needed when she was exposed to the outside existence beyond the Temple. This would involve leaving the main Atlantis Temple and travelling to the other eleven Temples as part of her development. She would witness at first-hand the failing utopia on Earth, and there was hope she could bring the light needed to these Temples to strengthen Atlantis again.

As you can imagine, I expressed my concern to my mission team that this seemed a lot to put on her shoulders. But they reminded me that her very being has already strengthened most of the priests' and priestesses' energies in the main light Temple, returning them into the light and higher love source without fear of what lay beyond the Temple walls. I also pointed out that she is already aware of the changes in Atlantis, as her sensitivity picks this up even through thick stone walls. I also realise that until she sees it first-hand, she will not fully connect to the feelings she has been experiencing. She has learnt to stay in the high vibration, keeping the negative energies at her boundaries. The test will be whether or not she can maintain this when she ventures out into the Earth world.

Aigle has been aware from a young age that she had an incarnated soul which came from a far-off planet. It was not until recently that she grasped she could communicate with this being she is connected to. Because she has built up her telepathic and clairvoyant skills to a high standard, she is now able to communicate with fellow humans at this level of development, as well as with her multidimensional guardians.

She has achieved this by setting the intent in a meditation to make the connection with her truth, her higher self. Through this, she managed to project herself through mind thought to a higher-level energy plane in the fourth dimension multidimensional energy space. This is where we met for the first time. She could see me through her third eye as a mind vision, as I am in my physical energy form. She asked me for a message of guidance. I chose to say, *"You have great purpose on Earth and you will bring the unconditional love and light needed to many who are slipping into the darkness and shadows of the lower energy".* When she came out of meditation I felt an uplift in her energies and she shed tears of joy as a result of the union of unconditional love energies that had just taken place. As for me it was an amazing experience, as if I was seeing her form in front of me; I could feel my reflective self was part of her, my personality was her, but there was an individual human essence there as well. I just wanted to reach out and touch her and explore this human form, as she was much more than I expected, but I knew it was a projection of her energy and not solid physical form. Even so, I felt much love for her.

When I view my life with her through my reflective self it is not the same sensation. I know I sense, feel and see all she does, but there is a detachment of feelings when I watch her life. When we met in the fourth dimension energy, there was a more heartfelt connection for Aigle. I now see the human essence of her, the mind, body and individual human spirit, her dreams and feelings, with my reflective self-being part of her as well. I asked Avilil what would happen to all this when her life on Earth ends. He said as with all physical forms that are not capable of ethereal body and multidimensional form, the body will go back to its original form – for Aigle, this means Earth. Her physical energy and life energy are taken back to Mother Earth and stays connected to her and the creation link in the twelfth dimension, until the day Earth is called back to the womb of creation. My reflective self will hold the memories, feelings and the essence of that human, which will stay with me for my physical existence. When my physical body is no longer needed, my multidimensional form will retain all this as well. Every incarnation lives on in the being that chooses to incarnate, and they are never the same again. They evaluate their past physical life, carrying forward the positive energy and healing from the negative vibrations that physical life might have left on their ethereal being. Avielil had tried to explain to me what incarnation would be like when we started this mission, but I have to admit, you have to experience it, as words will never do it justice.

Another outcome of this new connection with me is that her other guardians, Telcarian, Ioliismiem and Avielil have also been able to draw closer to her energy field and she has been picking up on their thoughts and guidance to her questions. This means we can now all influence her thoughts to guide her on her life's path when she asks us for help.

I must add the other discussion we had this light day, that we all sensed her concern about certain individuals around in the Temple. Even though we all felt the energy had improved there were still energies that were worrying her. The priest called Guildan was still there and Aigle would sometimes see him, watching her in the shadows. She had not expressed her concern to any other Earth being as she thought perhaps she was imagining this feeling of fear from him – after all, he is a high-ranking priest in the Temple of Light. She would sometimes sense that something was watching her, but she had learnt to block out this negative feeling, as it could affect her day-to-day energies. She did wonder if she was picking up on the lower energies influencing other humans creating the ego and karma energy. She could not put a finger on it, and trusted – as did we – that in time all would be revealed.

Life Journal – transmission 47 -
'The light within Atlantis'

The Atlantic mission had now become one of the top priorities for the Intergalactic Council, because the experiment was failing. I found out from my father that more light beings from the Intergalactic Council were coming to Diacurat because of this. It seemed that one of their areas of focus was me and the progress Aigle was making. There were thousands of incarnated souls on Earth so the fact mine was so important made me realise that this was a tipping point for the experiment. As yet, nothing had been confirmed in the presence of the mission team, but I felt they were close to ending the Atlantis experiment. I was finding this hard to comprehend, but having studied the history of the other four experiments, it seemed that, unless there was a miracle, this would be the eventual outcome.

I chose to keep this information and feelings to myself, and focus on the task in hand. I had less private time now as Aigle's life and actions were such a high priority to everyone. I had to keep up with my connection all the while so nothing was missed, and guidance could be given through my reflective self and her guardians.

Aigle had reached her sixteenth year and as we planned, the time came for her to meet the Celestial Guardians. The first meeting was held in the domed initiation chamber. The high priest and priestess were there with a few other high-ascended masters. The twelve beings transported themselves in to the room. I could feel Aigle's anticipation and excitement, and she was in awe when they appeared. To her they looked like rays of bright light all showing their individual colours, and as they moved there were wisps of energy behind them which she thought looked like wings. She also realised she had seen these beings in her dreams and as a child she had tried to draw them in her art, portraying them in human form with large wings, trying to express what she had seen. When, as a child, she had asked about these beings, she was told they were the Twelve Celestial Guardians of Atlantis.

She was introduced to them one by one, starting with *Light of Communication* – colour astral blue ray, *Light of Grace Within* – colour fire red ray, *Light of Connection* – colour star yellow ray, *Light of Teaching* – colour translucent ray, *Light of Truth* – colour violet ray, *Light of Healing* – colour emerald ray, *Light of Knowledge* – colour indigo ray, *Light of Energy* – colour amber ray, *Light of Order* – colour lilac ray, *Light of Presence* – colour pink ray, *Light of Comfort* – colour azure ray and *Light of Love* – colour silver ray.

The Celestial Guardians use telepathic communication of the Earth language with the Atlanteans. The *light of teaching* being stepped forward to communicate with Aigle, and explained their purpose, the star ship and the crystals that power Atlantis. They also complimented her on her dedication to her learning and understanding of her Earth journey. They explained that if she had not developed to such a high level of ascension they could not have been able to link with her on this stage of her Earth journey. They also felt it was time for her to know the full extent of the failing Atlantis experiment. With her inner light, as with many others at this ascended level, they held hope that if they walked among the Atlanteans, they would see the error of their ways. This would involve the priests and priestesses travelling from the main Temple from city to city, giving their messages of love and healing to those who needed it from the Temple sources. They explained the chosen priests and priestesses would have to keep their high ascended energy at all times and protect themselves from the manifesting lower energies destroying the utopia that had been created. They felt if they worked in unison there was still hope for the Atlantean humans, and while there is hope you never give up.

The Celestial Guardians then returned to their star ship to leave Aigle to reflect on their message to her and the others present.

Life Journal – transmission 48 -
'The light within Atlantis'

There have been further meetings with the Celestial Guardians about the Atlantis experiment. They have also met with the Intergalactic Council, which feeds back to all species that are involved in the Atlantis incarnation programme. The result of these meetings is they have all agreed on the way forward – that the priests and priestesses will journey through the Atlantean cities. They feel this will be the last attempt to enhance the energies of Atlantis and is a positive strategy to try and turn around the experiment.

Finally the Earth day came for Aigle to start her journey with the chosen priests and priestesses, drawn from all of the Temples across Atlantis, travelling together across the lands and spreading the word of unconditional love to all they came across.

I could feel Aigle's excitement and her open heart trusting the journey would be what Atlantis needed, bringing the guiding light to those who had fallen from their path of light. She has such an innocent, trusting heart that I felt concerned for her, as I suspect this journey will bring more than she could prepare for and imagine at her moment in Earth time. As bystanders, we were anticipating both the positives and pitfalls that could happen on this journey, but of course, this was never relayed to her in case it triggered the negative doubt energy that could affect her work.

The journey to bring more of the unconditional light source to Atlantis started in the main city itself, with the procession walking round it and talking to its people. Some were given healing or guided to follow them in this quest of bringing a higher energy source back to the people – to be used for the whole not the self. The first thing Aigle noticed were scattered empty dwellings, which had belonged to the people who had become materialistic, developed ego and karma energy, and caused problems amongst the population. The priests and priestesses invited people to mass gatherings of meditation and healing, giving guidance on the importance of connecting to the higher source energy and working for the whole to survive. They worked hard on building the energy back up in the city and out into the countryside surrounding it. By the time they moved to the next city, they could feel the higher energies were already stronger again. They hoped that as each city made this transformation, the energy would link up around Earth, bringing the higher energy back to the forefront of the Atlantian people's existence.

I found out this light day from Avielil that many people had used the pool of healing light at the Light Temples to keep themselves healed and in the high-energy source. But some Earth time ago, some started to realise its power, and that it could be used for their own ambitions. This led to them using it for self-enhancement to create dominance over others; this changed their behaviour, which worked for the self, not the whole. These people were asked to leave the community only as a last resort. Many had tried to work with them to bring them back into the higher energies, but it was unsuccessful. There seemed to be a barrier with some humans once they had shifted into the lower energies. These humans had to be taken away from those who were still trying to work in the high energy, but even they now had that inner doubt energy seeping in, which was causing them to waver.

As this light mission from Atlantis travelled round Earth to each city, they found the same situation in each place. Aigle and many others felt it was worth the time to raise the energies as it was helping the cities, but she felt they should be visiting the dwelling places that had been created by the people who had left the Atlantis society, to try and bring them back into the light. She discussed this with the high priestesses and priests, as she felt this was the only way to save Atlantis. A meeting was called with the Celestial Guardians and on reflection, they also felt this was a journey they should all make.

I had been observing this journey from city to city and taking in all the architecture for Zogica's interest. The Temple where they held the meeting with the Celestial Guardian beings was set up high on a large plateau. They had travelled overland in their powered hover vehicles. These vehicles are powered by crystals and the Earth's light star. The Temple has a healing pyramid but the main structure was made of very large columns of T-shaped square pillars set in circles, with ornate covered rooms set off at different angles. At the centre there was a healing fountain and pool and the Temple crystal, which was guarded by the Celestial Guardian *Light of Knowledge,* who oversaw this Temple and its teachings.

I had observed that each Temple was completely different in its architecture. The one thing they had in common were pyramid structures for dwellings or healing, while some had both. The architecture was built for the purpose it would serve and the type of energy it was required to pulsate out to Earth. Another Temple that was quite magnificent was built to align with the light star and Earth's moon, harnessing their energies. The Celestial Guardian *Light of Energy* oversaw this Temple. It was set at the centre of the city in a huge, lush valley, and was a large, layered pyramid with steps up each side and an entrance off the steps. Inside were the light pool of healing and many rooms for meditation, healing and teaching. The city was spread out into the valley where there was a second pyramid for healing, which channelled the moon's energy. As Aigle entered the healing pyramid she could feel it was a very powerful source of energy. They all chose to spend a couple of days in this healing space to rejuvenate their energies, as they did at all the Temples' healing locations.

The Temple that Aigle liked the most was the one set in a valley at the mouth of a large river that divided into two just before the city. There were three pyramids aligned with the distant stars, where the Celestial Guardian *Light of Communication* resided. The main Temple pyramid was the largest of the three and held the healing pool and crystal. The other two combined to enhance healing energy and communication to off-world sources such as the Intergalactic Council star ships and star gates. The walls of the Temples were painted with murals, reflecting Atlantean history in beautiful art.

Like Atlantis city, this city was a travelling portal for observing visitors of the experiment. They were not seen; remember how I observed planets during multidimensional travelling, by being invisible to the planet's species. This was extended to Earth, where off-world visitors needed permission from the Intergalactic Council and the Celestial Guardians. This was the second largest city in the Atlantean empire, and was spread over several miles, with many smaller energy-healing pyramids among the people's dwellings.

Zogica loved my descriptions of what we have observed through Aigle, but he would have to wait for the transmissions to be loaded to the planet's library to observe them fully himself. We can link with each other's minds to retrieve images and memories, but I am not allowed to let others view my links with my reflective self. It is all right for me to reveal basic knowledge but not what's going on in the experiment itself – such as its potential failure. It is hard keeping this from Zogica, as we are so close, but he never asks so that makes it easier for me. My parents are also aware of the possible failure, as they work with the dignitaries and some of the mission team. I can reflect with them when I get the chance, but it's been a while since I have had the moments to do this.

Life Journal – transmission 49 -
'The light within Atlantis'

As you probably realise from my transmissions, my life has been so focused on the Atlantic mission that my personal life is on hold so to speak. I am in the mission chamber all light day, and sometimes part of the dark night. Due to this high commitment level, I was struggling to look after Glitle, so Zogica has taken over until I can commit to her the time she needs. I am starting my light days with an extensive meditation with the intention to keep my energies fully balanced, which is working well, followed by a wonderful breakfast before going off to the mission chamber.

Up to now, I have usually been on my own in the chamber, with others monitoring when they choose to log in to my transmission recordings. But now I have Telcarian, Ioliismiem and Avielil with me so we can bring the energy, healing and guidance as needed to Aigle without interruption.

While Aigle has been on the journey to help bring the unconditional light source back to Atlantis, I have seen her grow in inner self and power. She came into her own when interacting with the people of Atlantis city, and just her presence brought calmness and healing to those she met. She has a natural rapport with people; she can immediately sense their concerns and weaknesses and can focus her energies to help them. She could fully balance those who were still in the high energies but were struggling with them, by healing their chakras and auras. She worked to heal the physical bodies of others who had started to falter, and perhaps had some physical illness symptoms as a result. She also tried to lead them back to meditation and the mindfulness needed to restore clarity. The people would then need to take responsibility for themselves, with guidance from those left behind at the Temple. This is because Aigle and the other priests and priestesses would be absent as they journeyed around the cities of Atlantis.

Aigle had a vision for Atlantis to be healed, and trusted in these beautiful humans she had encountered so far. I realised she had no doubt that all would be OK as she only had a vision of a reunited utopia, once again for all. She also knew that her companions on the journey shared this thinking. There was one dark cloud – she had spoken to me, her higher self, about her concerns about the priest Guildan, and had asked for guidance. He appeared to shine in the light to all the others, but she saw darkness and his energies were blocked to her. She still had not spoken to another Earth human about this but it was in her thoughts often now. We saw this was a threat to her energies and mission on Earth.

I noticed that he always seemed to be allocated to her group in nearly everything she did, and he was very close to the high priestess Cardinea and her private circle of confidants. My guidance was that she talked to the high priestess and Celestial Guardians, which she was entitled to do. We felt she was one of the most intuitive humans we had seen; with her high penetrating powers, we felt she could see and sense something the others were not seeing. As this sense had started in her childhood and persisted, we knew she was not imagining it. She had always been able to sense when something was wrong with some people, and now she could see the energies that confirmed it. Through her meditation connection to us she heard our message, and we left it with her to decide what to do next.

Life Journal – transmission 50 -
'The light within Atlantis'

It took Aigle a few Earth days to mull over our advice on the priest Guildan. She was also finding it difficult to be alone with the high priestess Cardinea without him being there. But patience paid off and one day when they were all getting ready to leave the last Temple and travel back to Atlantis City, she found Cardinea who was on her own in her chamber packing. Aigle asked if she could speak to her, requesting that they walked in the Temple gardens, away from unseen prying eyes and ears.

Aigle chose to open up to Cardinea about her feelings as a child about this priest, as well as a couple of other people who had concerned her as she was growing up, such as Irinea, the lady who helped her mother. She explained that she could not read Guildan's aura and saw dark energy like no other she had encountered in a human form. The only way she could explain it was that it was not of Earth, an energy not seen before in Atlantis that she recognised. Cardinea asked if it was possible that she was sensing the incarnated soul and was confused by it, but even as she spoke the words, she knew it could not be the case. Aigle had now encountered many humans and could sense that the incarnated souls from high dimensions of love and light were pure energy. Aigle replied, *"This is different. It is something we cannot see and is shrouded from us, I am convinced of this."* Cardinea knew she could not dismiss this, as Aigle had proved to be one of the most highly ascended intuitive humans yet to be born within this fifth Atlantis experiment, and it could be she had a sense something the rest had not. Cardinea finally agreed that they should meet with the Celestial Guardian being *Light of Communication* to discuss this.

Cardinea arranged to take Aigle to the star ship for the meeting, before their journey home. She told no one and asked Aigle not to tell anyone where she was going and what was being discussed. The high priestess wanted the matter looked into by the Celestial Guardians, then addressed by the Intergalactic Council if there was a problem.

A couple of Earth days later, the Celestial Guardians transported them to their star ship into a room adapted to an Earth air chamber atmosphere. I could actually feel Aigle's nerves and excitement, as it was only the highest ranking that liaised in this way with the Celestial Guardians. Celestial Guardian being *Light of Communication* listened to Aigle's concerns. I could sense her fear that they might dismiss her worries, but she had no need to worry.

The guardian explained they were observing closely the energy changes in the human forms who had moved away from the light ascension energy; they had found some who had caused concern but had not yet revealed this to anyone. He explained that when a human form develops ego, doubt and karma, their energy changes and can be seen as a lower, darker, heavier energy; they no longer shine bright and their soul and aura seem duller. They had found among these observations there were a few that had shown an even darker energy which seemed to shroud the soul energy from them. But they had not had any reason yet to look at the humans that were believed to be living in the light and seen as the light by others. They praised Aigle for her sensibility in coming forward with this and asked her to remain silent on the subject. They respected her ability and powers and felt this backed up their own findings. They will investigate this further and come back when they have something to discuss.

My mission team found all this fascinating, and we wondered, what was this energy that Aigle was observing? Questions were being asked and others were offering their own opinions but we knew better than to jump to conclusions. We all had to wait to see what was concluded from the guardians observations, and whether Aigle would see any further energy changes.

Meanwhile, after a Earth year of travelling the lands of Earth to the Atlantean cities, the specially chosen group was travelling back to Atlantis to assess their progress and plan the next journey to the fallen Atlantean communities.

Life Journal – transmission 51 -
'The light within Atlantis'

On the return to Atlantis city Aigle was nearing the end of her seventeenth year, and yet again we had seen a big change in her development and a new maturity. She had gained this in two ways, firstly from the human side where she had acquired a greater understanding of other humans and had a mature empathy with them. Secondly, her understanding of her powers and how powerful she actually was, had grown with her intuition, clairvoyance and telepathic development, as well as the sixth sense of her deep ascension knowledge. With this new maturity came an inner strength, so that she no longer doubted herself. As you know from my earlier transmissions, the doubt energy is a very powerful negative energy which stops us all achieving our full potential.

The group of travelling priests and priestesses all chose to return to the main Atlantis city to evaluate their progress with the guardians and recharge their energies before the next phase of their mission. Aigle was so happy to see her parents and the members of her family who were still in Atlantis. During this time of rest and reflection Aigle was elevated to a higher priestess status, in recognition of her powers and the good works she had achieved so far. What this meant for her was that supervision was no longer needed and she could now teach and guide others on their Temple spiritual journey. I have to admit she took all this in her stride – it was just a title after all; she was still her true self, with so much love for others.

They decided to rest for one of Earth's months, and give people time to see loved ones again. The priests and priestesses from other Temples returned to their homes to carry on with the good work achieved so far and was to return when called upon by the Celestial Guardians.

Aigle and some of the others from her Temple took this time to revisit the people of Atlantis city and reiterate what guidance they had given them a year ago, before they left on their travels. They were shocked to see more empty homes among the city dwellings, as they thought they had lifted the energy efficiently to stop this. Aigle was told some families had heard there was a better way of being, with abundance in materialistic form that would provide a certain future for them, and they had left to join those townships that were their next destination. She felt the energies had slipped back again, causing renewed unrest in the Atlantean people. They were seeing the failing utopia and felt their lives would be better elsewhere, and they were being fed false words of hope by the new powers over in the townships. She also knew these people's day-to-day powers were weakening as they slipped from the high ascension energies. The humans that used to teleport and use telekinesis to move objects were now few and far between in the city population. Further investigation revealed that the other cities were also finding this. This did not sit well with the mission team and the intergalactic members observing all of this on Earth.

For the moment, the Temples themselves were maintaining their high energy levels with the support of the Celestial Guardians. I could see Aigle was trying her best to hold her power and conviction to this cause to save Atlantis, but even she had the doubt energy creeping in too; it was like a disease sweeping the utopia of Earth. She was also aware that other high-ranking priests and priestesses were expressing doubt quietly to each other, and this seemed to be led by the priest Guildan. Aigle was asking us for guidance and we led her to keep confiding her concerns in Cardinea and the Celestial Guardians – as a means of clearing her energies, and to enable her guides and mentors to act.

Life Journal – transmission 52 –
'The light within Atlantis'

This light day started off with me and my mission team reflecting on Aigle and what had taken place recently in the Earth days of the Atlantic mission. The Celestial Guardians had met with the Intergalactic Council and the overseers to decide on actions to save the fifth Atlantis experiment. They decided to allow the second phase of trying to heighten the Earth's energies, by letting the chosen priests and priestesses go out to the townships of Atlantean people who had left the cities. The remaining priests and priestesses at each Temple and the Celestial Guardian would keep working on their individual cities to maintain the high energies needed to succeed.

It was also decided that the travelling group would have human guards to protect them. All the cities had human protectors who monitored the boundaries, keeping the cities safe from anything negative that would not serve them. The protectors are capable of telepathic materialisation and illusion to deter unwanted low energy humans and mammals from the city boundaries. They could either manifest something to deter unwanted humans, or create the illusion that the city was not there. Because the Celestial Guardians had sensed unrest in these outcast communities, which could threaten the safety of the travelling priests and priestesses, the decision was made to use protectors.

Before they left on this new journey, we observed Aigle meditating and working on her energy balance and self-healing. She was also wondering if the Celestial Guardian being of *Light of Communication* had found out more about the priest Guildan's energy, and why it was so different from that of other humans. I hoped it was resolved soon, as this would help Aigle's energies settle. I was working with my reflective self to help keep her balanced, but was aware of the uncertain energy surrounding her.

We had watched the Atlantis group leave the city for the first township; the journey took four Earth days to reach the destination, which was located south of the Atlantis city at the foot of a range of mountains. They traveled in their hover land crafts – I have already mentioned these but not explained the technology to you. Made from a cosmic metal material supplied to the Alanteans, they are flat crafts that move by vibration attuned to the individual telepathic human mind, supported by a crystal technology for control. The crafts vary in size, with capacity for anything from one or two passengers up to twenty-four, plus cargo. When Aigle travelled on these, I sensed she was a little unsure as for most of her life, she had moved about on foot in her Temple and her city surroundings, and had never travelled far until now.

They decided not stay in the township but instead, set up a camp a small distance outside it. The resting tents were pyramid-shaped and brightly coloured, and there were larger pyramid tents for eating and meditating. They stayed near water sources and had brought their own food, intending to gather what they needed as they travelled. The next Earth day they sent an emissary, a high priest called Antonio and a band of protectors, to meet the leader of the township to discuss the meaning of their visit. On his return he reported they were willing to meet and listen to a small party from their camp.

A group of twelve was selected, supported by protectors,

which included Aigle, Antonio and the priest Guildan. They chose to fly to the perimeter of the town and enter by foot, so they could observe the people and their energies. I can tell you this was quite an experience for Aigle and us as observers. This town had been built and added to for over one hundred and fifty Earth years. It was a lot more primitive and less ornate than the Atlantean cities, but this was because they had lost their abilities to materialise what they required, and had to build everything by hand. They also had to grow their own food source to survive, but recently had tried to raid food from the Atlanteans, as disease was consuming their own crops. Some of the humans looked diseased and there were signs of both great wealth and poverty. Aigle was shocked by what she saw; I felt her heart have a strong palpitation for the first time in her life as the energy of despair hit her, and it took everything she had to control her emotions.

A little boy came up to ask her for food, she gave him what she had on her and placed a healing hand on him. She sensed a lost soul within him and was confused by the human's choice. But she realised this child had no choice, as his parents had created this reality for him. She was trying to understand why some of humanity would choose this existence over a world of helping each other to create a utopia existence of one working for the whole.

There was a lot of curiosity as they made their way through the streets. When they reached the meeting place with the civic leaders, Aigle realised it was the most impressive building in the town. They were met by men who carried weapons, apparently for protection. Avielil told me that these weapons used a high-energy laser pulse technology that could kill a human. Amongst the Atlanteans who had moved to the townships were the scientists and technology experts who had created these powerful killing weapons. Even I was having trouble comprehending this because as a race, the Diacuratians had never created weapons to harm others.

The group was led into a hall where, at the far end, three men sat in chairs behind an ornate table. There were guards everywhere, as well as what appeared to be citizens of the township. I noticed from Aigle's reaction, feelings and thoughts that she could sense the negativity in the room. Antonio lead the discussions, basically saying why they were there, and how they wished the township to convert back to the high spiritual way of being and rejoin the Atlantean communities. He also explained that they were travelling the Earth to visit all Atlanteans who had left the main cities. The leader of the township seemed to find this all very amusing and said they would require food and riches from the Cities before they could consider their proposal.

Aigle quietly observed the room and to her surprise the three leaders had the same dark energy as the priest Guildan. She was asking us for strength and guidance at this time, so as she stood there observing we sent all the energy and healing we could to her. She felt our energy come round her and she focused on these three human leaders. She saw through their energy boundaries, and was surprised at what she felt. The energy that would be the incarnated soul was not of unconditional love and light. It was a negative, destructive energy, and there was no high ethereal ascension love soul in these humans. Her concentration was broken as she turned to see Guildan observing her; their eyes met and the moment stood still. She sensed that he knew what she had discovered, that she could see he was of the same energy she had observed with the three leaders.

Antonio closed the discussions and said they would return the next day with their answer to the proposal. They quietly left the town meeting hall and started out along the streets, but as they came into a square, they were suddenly surrounded by guards with weapons aimed at them. The citizens were gathering to see what was happening and there were shouts from the crowds telling them to leave and they were not wanted there. The leader of the guards said they were not free to go and had to return to the town meeting hall. The protectors acted quickly, creating the illusion of smoke and invisibility for the group, and they were able to run to the entrance of the township and escape on their flying hovercrafts. Many of them, including Aigle, were visibly shaken by this experience. They very quickly decided to return to the safety of Atlantis city, to report their findings and seek guidance from the Celestial Guardians.

The Guardians, of course, were already aware of these events, as they always observed everything from afar, and quickly went to the Intergalactic Council for guidance themselves. But they were not yet aware of what we had witnessed with Aigle, and the lower energies of the human leaders and Guildan.

Life Journal – transmission 53 –
'The light within Atlantis'

The journey back to Atlantis city was a time of reflection for the travelling group, as they all tried to conserve their energies and powers. They had all had a shock to their way of thinking, and were finding it hard to believe the way the behaviour of the township humans had degraded.

Aigle felt very uneasy, as she was holding on to the knowledge of the dark energy she had witnessed and did everything she could to avoid Guildan. He was outwardly behaving in the same ways as they all were, with shock and concern and comforting others, but we knew Aigle felt he was deceiving them all. She was biding her time so that on her return she could reveal to Cardinea and the Celestial Guardians what she had discovered.

I could feel her energies getting heavier and the doubt was now strong in her, the doubt of the success of saving the utopia she loved. I had to witness her crying to herself and praying for a good outcome. I felt her innocence had gone; she had not been prepared for this new Earth that had been shown to her. I felt there was a naivety in the Atlantis high status beings – and even the Celestial Guardians. I was trying to understand myself what was happening. Surely they knew what the outcome of this township meeting would be? The Guardians are all seeing and knowing, but this is an experiment, and experiments are about letting things run their course to achieve a true result. Once you have assessed the outcome, you can decide, based on the results, what further experiments can be carried out. I also found I was struggling with the logic of my scientific training against my emotions for this Earth being.

I took all of these recent events to my mission team, asking for Intergalactic Council representatives to be there. After I revealed the recent events in Aigle's life they adjourned the meeting and agreed they would return in a couple of light days with their reflections on these recent events in Atlantis.

I am very tired at the end of this light day so was glad to get back to my chamber to rest and reflect on what I had witnessed, and to meditate and correct my energies. I know my reflective self was trying to adjust to Aigle's energies, which was also affecting me. Zogica was at the Temple with my mother and he came to see me, I could not say much to him but he could see I was tired. He gave me a healing hug and said you know where I am if you need me. The mission team had agreed I should have a good dark night's rest and we would reconvene early in the next light day.

Life Journal – transmission 54 -
'The light within Atlantis'

I record this transmission with a shaky mind and energies as I have had not had many light days yet to adjust to the recent experiences and events I now reveal to you. I was resting in my chamber at the end of my previous transmission when I suddenly awoke and felt a strong imbalance; I had never felt like this before, as if I was going to black out. I was shaky and felt an energy vibration I had not experienced before and was unsure of what was happening. I sent my thoughts to Telcarian, Ioliismiem and Avielil that I was in trouble and they transported instantly to my chambers, and took me to the multidimensional incarnation chambers. We linked into Aigle and to my horror, there were no physical life signs. I could feel nothing of her and we soon realised that my reflective self had left the human body because Aigle had died. My imbalance of energy had happened at the earth moment of her death.

Avielil said they needed to multidimensional travel immediately to the Earth energies to retrieve my reflective self, escort it back to Diacurat, and re-link us as soon as possible. I was to stay in the chamber and split in to my multidimensional form and enter the light harmonic sound particle transmitter, ready to receive my reflective self back into my energy. What then seemed only moments later they returned with my reflective self-energy, which joined me in the harmonic sound particle transmitter. I felt the rotation of the energies and a pulsation as I had on the separation process, and when my multidimensional form was whole again I returned to my physical form and became unconscious.

I came round in a monitoring chamber and although I was

confused, I knew I was whole again. I wanted to ask lots of questions but was told to rest and sleep; when I was fully focused again, they would explain what happened to Aigle and me. I must have been quite out of reality, but I do remember seeing faces like my parents, Zogica, Telcarian, Ioliismiem and Avielil. I discovered they had all come to see me while I was recovering.

A couple of light days later I was strong enough to meet the mission team and find out what had happened to Aigle. There were also a couple of Intergalactic Council members at the meeting to reveal further outcomes from observations from the Atlantis experiment. It was good to hear what happened to Aigle as I could not feel her human link any more. It was confirmed she had died, poisoned by the priest Guildan. They revealed that he was the equivalent of a spy in Atlantis for the humans that had left the Atlantis cities, and held powerful positions in the new townships. The incarnated souls of these beings that Aigle had identified with the dark energies were not incarnated souls sent by the intergalactic team from the incarnation programme. They were from a physical ascension race that did not live in the high unconditional love energies. They thrived on negative energies, like ego, karma, war and disruption to other societies. This race was called Derepliticon from a physical planet also existing in star ships in the low multidimensional dimensions. They are very sophisticated and their technology is advanced. It was revealed they had been infiltrating the Atlantis experiments for possibly a very long time, causing disruptions to the high ascension energies, which in turn caused the humans to falter and descend into the lower heavier energies. They had managed to remain hidden as they had technology to disguise themselves from the high-energy love forms in the universe.

The revelation that this race was now thought to be the cause of all the experiments of Atlantis failing had rippled through the Intergalactic Council like a shock wave. They now had to go back through many hyons of recordings in the universal library to identify how and when they entered each experiment. Had they caused all of them to fail or was it just the fifth? The conclusion was they had discovered the first experiment after it had been going for thousands of Earth years, and then started their assault on each experiment, carefully choosing when to enter to avoid detection. Their aim was to cause the disruption and negative energy that they could thrive upon.

Aigle's clairvoyant powers and some unique inner knowing had revealed them to her, even though she did not understand what they were. The priest Guildan saw her as a threat to their existence, that she would reveal them, and on this basis decided she needed to be eliminated to protect their disguise. He added a poison to a fruit drink that was taken to her Temple chamber for her; she innocently drank it and death was instantaneous. As this happened when I was not observing her, my reflective self had no choice but to leave the body protected by the Celestial Guardians and wait for us to arrive and take it back home. The jolt I experienced out of my resting time and the way I felt was the result of this. When I sent the alert to Telcarian, Ioliismiem and Avielil, they all tuned into Aigle straightaway, realised something was very wrong, and acted quickly to protect me.

My mission as an incarnated soul was over and at once, I felt lost and emotional. I reflected on whether I could have done more? Would it have made a difference if I had been observing her at the time? I now know it would not have, as they let the physical life live its course, observing, guiding and learning as the observer. I knew why Aigle was born into Atlantis and her life mission was to bring hope and a light to the lower energies. She was yet another hope for the experiment, and they had many in place, but it was not enough anymore. I asked if the Celestial Guardians had foreseen this outcome and why Aigle had not sensed that her life, and the lives of others, were in danger. I now realise the humans had an innocence of trust from only seeing the good in everything. This was because of all the years of living in a utopian society created this positive way of thinking. They had not been prepared for these lower heavy energies, or understand that they could do harm to others. Because the Derepliticon race had mastered the art of disguising their incarnated soul energies, no one was looking for it, and it had been missed. This scenario had not even crossed anyone's mind in all the years of the Atlantis experiments, but now it was all starting to make sense.

I realised I had made an emotional attachment to Aigle I had not expected. We are not a cold race, it's simply that over many hyons, we have controlled our feelings to help our ascension process. I had grown to care about this human I was part of, and had started to understand the humanoid existence. I could see a physical form that, if given the chance, could ascend as we have and would not need an incarnated host to bring the love and light to their world. I hoped that humanity could have that one day on Earth.

I have further reflections to discuss but for now will rest and take moments to heal and reflect on the final events of the mission.

Life Journal – transmission 55 –
'The light within Atlantis'

I am feeling more balanced now, after a few light days of healing and meditating with the help of my mother in the Temple meditation chambers. I just wanted to add to this journal section more recent events on the Atlantis experiment. I will soon conclude this part of my journal, returning to my normal life journal transmissions. As I said in the first transmission, 'The light within Atlantis' will be held in the universal library, but only those given permission by the Intergalactic Council can connect to it. On my death of physical form, my life journal will be assessed; if suitable, it will be released for all to learn from. I have no idea what the rest of my life will entail, but I am hoping it will be remarkable enough to help and guide others on their life's path.

I had my final meeting yesterday with my team for the Atlantis mission. The intergalactic ascension master Fedrycon had especially come to meet us. It soon became apparent why he was there; it was to welcome us to the incarnation programme and enlighten us on the outcome of the fifth Atlantis experiment. The Diacuratians had agreed to enter the incarnation programme with a selected few from our planet, in the hope more will then be involved. Fedrycon started the meeting by thanking us for all our hard work and dedication. He told us we had made a valuable contribution, and much had been learned from Aigle's life and our observations. He confided that after great deliberation among the overseers, Intergalactic Council and Celestial Guardians, they had decided to end the fifth Atlantis experiment.

He updated us with further details; on the death of Aigle, the priest Guildan had escaped the Temple as he had been exposed as the killer. The energies in all the cities had carried on declining with not much hope of recovery – the balance of lower, heavy energies now outweighed the lighter love energies. The star races involved in the incarnation programme had all agreed that it should end. They had been given the choice to trigger the death of the physical host and collect their incarnated reflective selves, or carry on in the physical form until a natural death occurred on Earth. They had also decided not to do another Atlantis experiment on Earth; the result of this decision would mean that all their powers, crystals, technology and the Celestial Guardians would leave the planet. They also wanted to destroy any buildings using Atlantis technology so it was not handed to any future Earth occupation or experiment that might be influenced by it. They asked the humans that chose to stay to vacate the cities to high ground, and then created Earthquakes that triggered tsunamis, taking the land and the evidence of Atlantis back to the depths of the seas.

The humans left on Earth that survived these huge floods of waters would be left alone for a few Earth centuries to survive and evolve naturally. The Salcaritons would still incarnate any newborn humans, trying to maintain some sort of balance for Earth among the humanoid forms. All the others involved would step back from the incarnation programme on Earth, but would stay as guardians of the planet.

I asked about the Derepliticon race and what actions were being taken against them to prevent this happening anywhere else in the universe. He said the Arcturians, Pleiadians and Andromedans would now have the Derepliticon energy signature from the Atlantis experiment; they would be able to identify them and put a strategy in place to stop their star ships travelling the universe cosmos to cause disruption and destruction.

I also enquired about the future role of the Celestial Guardians of Atlantis. He told us they would always have a connection with Earth and be supporting the Salcaritons. They might choose to incarnate in a future timeline of Earth to help aid humanity ascend. As to when this will be has yet to be decided – if at all – but the moments of our reality will one day reveal the outcome of this future story.

I also asked what Earth's future would be in his eyes, and the intergalactic view on this unique planet. He felt there would be future interaction on Earth, and there are plans to increase the human population around the planet, using the DNA that is left in the humans now there. Their DNA will revert to a lower energy stranded DNA and their chakras will close down. The safeguard built into the DNA will one day be retriggered when the time is right, with high-ascended masters and beings being incarnated again alongside the Salcaritons to aid humanity's ascension. They know it will be hard but it's possible to create a humanoid race that will self ascend as we have, in common with many other planets and civilisations.

Where there is hope there are possibilities, he reminded us. I felt he was a very wise being and perhaps one day, I will see the results of a positive Earths future. For now, though, it's time to say goodbye to some of my mission friends, but knowing we will meet again soon.

Life Journal – transmission 56 –
'The light within Atlantis'

As I sit in my new dwelling contemplating my future, I am filled with even more joy and excitement than usual. I have had the healing that I needed after my incarnation experience with Aigle on planet Earth. The process included detaching from any negative experiences I absorbed from Aigle's life and reflecting on the guidance I gave her while on her Earth journey. This healing was carried out in group work with Telcarian, Ioliismiem and Avielil, as they were her guides as well, and gave me group and individual energy healing. Avielil informed me that this is what all incarnated beings go through after this experience. It is a process of learning from the wisdom and knowledge gained from the experience, and taking forward what will benefit others.

I did feel wiser and had been asked if it was an experience I would wish to repeat. After some reflection I thought I would, as I would understand the process better and my experience with Aigle would help any future choices I made in a similar situation.

I am now bonded with Zogica and we have moved into our new home, which is beautiful. It is built from a shimmering crystal substance and is very spacious with lots of natural light. The home faces the lake and is a wonderful relaxing environment with a veranda to sit out on, where we can admire all that is around us. He has also built me a pyramid-healing chamber as I saw used in the Atlantis times, and he has his creative flow space as well.

As I sit here with Glitle on my lap reflecting on my life, I am looking at the images of the bonding ceremony and remembering that wonderful light day and night. We did gain permission to have it at the Temple in the sacred light room, and had the use of the gardens for the reception afterwards. All our families and friends were there, and my brother made it back from a mission to attend, which was wonderful. I was so happy that light day, and I will always hold the memories and love in my heart. Life is good for us both and we feel the time we spent apart while I was involved in the Atlantis experiment strengthened us. It has strengthened our love and devotion for each other, and as individuals, we found our true paths. Zogica's path is designing homes and creating beautiful public spaces, and mine is with my scientific background, working with the multidimensional energies and teaching ascension process and healing. Now we have joined the incarnation programme, I will also be involved with those that participate from our planet, and their healing process afterwards.

There are so many future possibilities but for now I am happy to enjoy the moment and let my life force flow as it should in the unconditional love that surrounds me.

I send blessings to all that connect to my transcripts of 'The light in Atlantis' and hope it gives you the light you need to find your true self and your own utopia.

… Transmission ends

About the Author

Sharon Milne Barbour from Bengalrose Healing is a medium and holistic healer based in Newport, South Wales (UK). Through her work with spirit, she loves to help people find happiness and healing by raising their positive energy levels with messages from loved ones in spirit. Her passion is also to teach others about the spiritual path and mediumship. Her seventh book, *'The light within Atlantis*, follows on from her previous books, *'Utopia - The Magic of Spirit' - 'The Magic of Words' - 'Ayderline the Spirit Within' - 'Step into the Mind of a Medium' - 'Heavenly Guidance'* and *'Inspiration Guidance Cards'*.

Sharon's books are available on Amazon, as well as from her own website: www.bengalrose.co.uk.

Visit her website www.bengalrose.co.uk to find out more about Sharon.

You can also find her on twitter @SBengalrose and FaceBook Bengalrosehealing.

Sharon has a YouTube channel with over one hundred spiritual guidance videos. Search 'Sharon Bengalrose'.

Sharon also welcomes contact through email: Sharon@bengalrose.co.uk.

Printed in Great Britain
by Amazon

35291737R00127